Praise for Samuel Fisher

'*Migraine* is a beguiling, sinuous wonder of a novel.
Simultaneously a work of intimate psychogeography, and a
mystery unravelling the interlacing breakdowns of climate,
health and domestic coupledom, I didn't want it to end'
Daisy Lafarge on *Migraine*

'Generous, sharp and uplifting – hope refracts around
every page as we are taken beyond the apocalypse, and into the
recovery that comes next. Though so much has been stripped
away, the bedrock of Fisher's London endures – vital and steady,
and with it so do the precious rags of culture, friendship, love
and forgiveness. I felt the future rehumanise as I read through –
I love, and will never grow tired of, Sam Fisher's unbroken city'
Ben Pester on *Migraine*

'Stunning, insightful, deeply humane prose . . .
Fisher indicts all of us yet still offers hope that
we may change the ending of this story'
Olivia Sudjic on *Wivenhoe*

'Quiet, fable-like menace radiates from every page of
Wivenhoe. Elegant and searching, it asks vital questions
about what it means to be part of a community'
Sophie Mackintosh on *Wivenhoe*

'An elegantly terrifying narrative that is reminiscent
of Graham Swift's *Waterland* in its focus on an insular,
secretive community in the east of England'
Observer review on *Wivenhoe*

'Eerie and disorientating, visceral and elusive. I felt safe
yet scared. Such skilful and sensory storytelling'
Ashley Hickson-Lovence on *Wivenhoe*

Also by Samuel Fisher

The Chameleon
Wivenhoe

MIGRAINE

SAMUEL FISHER

corsair

CORSAIR

First published in Great Britain in 2025 by Corsair

1 3 5 7 9 10 8 6 4 2

A CIP catalogue record for this book
is available from the British Library.

HB ISBN: 978-1-4721-5828-4

Typeset in Dante by M Rules
Printed and bound in Great Britain by
Clays Ltd, Elcograf S.p.A.

Papers used by Corsair are from well-managed forests
and other responsible sources.

Corsair
An imprint of
Little, Brown Book Group
Carmelite House
50 Victoria Embankment
London EC4Y 0DZ

The authorised representative
in the EEA is
Hachette Ireland
8 Castlecourt Centre
Dublin 15, D15 XTP3, Ireland
(email: info@hbgi.ie)

An Hachette UK Company
www.hachette.co.uk

www.littlebrown.co.uk

FOR L & D

'We saw for a moment laid
out among us the body of
the complete human being
whom we have failed to
be, but at the same time,
cannot forget.'

VIRGINIA WOOLF,
The Waves

I like to run.

I like the slippery relation it holds you in, to the world you move through. Slow enough to take in your surroundings, but fast enough that you avoid becoming part of them.

I always preferred the pavements to the parks. Even before the Freeze, when Victoria Park and London Fields were filled with people on a Saturday morning dodging terriers and flat-white-laden strollers, I chose to dance instead around bus stops and fruit stalls, delivery vans and cyclists.

I had a domain, a little square mile of the city I thought of as my own. Dalston Lane, Mare Street, Hackney Road and Kingsland Road: the four points of my tilted compass. I made a labyrinth of all the curving streets in between. Before the snow, I could navigate head down by the cracks in the pavement, keeping a constantly refined internal map – every new florist with a name like a twee private detective agency, every natural wine bar and the pubs they replaced. What was the point, I always thought, of living in the city, if you couldn't carry it inside you. If your breath didn't mark a living record.

After the Thaw, when the migraines started for most, but not for me, I tied up my laces and began the process of rebuilding my map and my muscles.

Cracks had become fissures. Shops gutted, their innards strewn across the pavement in the time of uncertainty and panic; raw meat and underwear and scented candles preserved under the vitrine of ice were now revealed to assault the senses, until they were swept away by one of the storms.

Hackney Road was desolate. The procession of weekenders who crossed it juggling half-dead houseplants from Columbia Road with sourdough loaves from Broadway Market were gone for good. When the flower sellers stopped showing and the bakeries shuttered, the shops folded, the houses emptied. It taught us which communities were incidental, a collision of commerce and geography, and which ones had a stronger hold on the landscape, their roots anchored deeper in archaeological time.

Amid the desolation, signs of life. As Victoria Park filled up with drifters and spiritualists, the nail bars on Mare Street reopened, trading manicures. I ran past these travellers, wild-eyed and filthy with gleaming French tips. Turkish restaurants came back to life, serving hot, floury lahmacun, with 'real' lamb, a claim they had never felt the need to make before.

On Dalston Square, the first vertical farm in Hackney appeared. At the start, these farms were haphazard constructions:

a few scrounged solar panels and trays of lettuces to garnish the meagre aid parcels that had kept us alive since the snow began, but over time they became more organised. A simple principle developed: turning up for work – to split the seedlings, harvest the trays that had matured – meant you could take fruits of your labour home with you. It was a protest against our dependency on aid that developed into something else – a way of coming back together.

Kids that had used grow lights and hydroponics to grow weed in their bedrooms were now supervising the growth of leafy greens and grains. The whole block had been covered in scaffolding, erected to replace the flammable cladding that encased the building, a job that had never even been started. Sections that collapsed under the weight of the snow were repaired. On a fine day the place was a hive of activity, people scrabbling up and down the sides of the block, hoisting bags of compost.

I joined up, chipped in. Like everyone else, I was looking for something like redemption. I hoped these might be first green shoots.

Because who knew why the gulf stream dropped?

Who knew why the prevailing winds changed? Why the balance shifted, out over the Pacific Ocean between those sibling cyclonic systems, that marshalled the seasons around the globe.

Who knew why the snow fell, and didn't stop? Who knew why, after five years, it finally did? Why it brought with it these storms.

Who knew who was to blame for these headaches?

Well, we *knew*. We all knew. But it's one thing to know something in your mind, another to carry it in your body.

So, when the Thaw came, I was slow to notice. A new sound,

first. A creaking, as the ice began to groan. A trickle as, under the still-placid surface of the drifts, the water began to flow. From under the cosmetic alterations we had wrought, the tattoo of the city, the landscape made itself known. The water traced these old bones. It ran, as ever. Towards the river.

It ran off the broken rooftops and out of the broken shop-fronts, over the broken pavements and into the broken sewers. It ran through the packed earth, through the tunnels and plague pits, into the tributaries we had buried and paved over.

The smell came with the meltwater, when it began to unearth what had been buried by the snow. It was a sense that had atrophied. I had grown so used to my own scent that I had ceased to notice it. Everything else was supressed by the cold and carried away by the wind that brought in the snow to deposit.

Now, suddenly, everything was ripe. Everything rancid.

There were things I wasn't ready to face. So, I laced up my shoes and ran. After you and I got together, I ran more. After you left, even more.

You know all this, of course. You've been here all along. But it's hard to find an entry point – to pinpoint the beginning of the end of things between us.

As a kid, I always resented spending time with people who bored me, because they forced me to confront something about myself: a certain impatience, a lack of generosity. Now I resented people who threw into relief my able-bodiedness, because they made me confront the urge – barely supressed – to turn this to my advantage.

I was terrified of frailty, disgusted by it. Running was a way to outstrip this feeling. Mare Street, Hackney Road, Kingsland Road, Dalston Lane. And all the roads between.

I liked to listen to the *Shipping Forecast*. In the depths of the

Freeze, when I couldn't sleep, I was searching through my cache of BBC broadcasts when I came across the archive, stretching back twenty years. It was one of those cosy, esoteric cultural trinkets that had been swept away overnight. A soothing, gentle lapping of words and sounds: directions, back through time, to a place that no longer exists.

Initially I used the recordings when I couldn't sleep, but I took to listening to them on my runs because it made me feel like a traveller, from this antique land. Simply passing through.

*

I was on one of these spiralling circuits, three months after you left, halfway home as I turned onto Kingsland Road, when my first migraine came on.

Nothing could have prepared me for the all-conquering strangeness. My tongue, tending heavier, was weighted metallic. The world, a little closer, leaned brighter. And everything smelled like the Thaw: acrid and astringent and perfumed. All at once ripe fruit and paint stripper. There was a giddiness, buffeted by a rising panic, as the lights – are they lights? or absences banded with light – whirled in my periphery, casting out all doubt as to what was happening to me.

Words unravelled, floating free. I didn't anticipate meaning's loss of means to attach. There was numbness. MODERATE OR GOOD, OCCASIONALLY POOR. Or perhaps pain followed by its immediate absence: in my fingertips, licking its way up the ring finger of my right hand, strobing in and out as it wrapped around my forearm.

The searing came with jaw clench unclench disbelief, rooting my temple with the first hint of wind. A gasp, an insuck.

WARNING OF GALES IN VIKING, DOGGER, THAMES, DOVER.

It was too much. Already, too much. More to come, and worse, from everything I've heard. Sensations rebounding like rippling waves, running over one another. HUMBER, THAMES, DOVER, WIGHT WESTERLY, FIVE TO SEVEN.

Get inside. A directive issued from somewhere beneath the language that'd been lost as the wind's held breath released.

Too far from home. GOOD, OCCASIONALLY POOR. Too far for the pain and the weather and nausea that came next, with the wind's directive, as it tore at my clothes.

Buildings all boarded or – unboarded – unsafe. And the pain was a hot welt, no longer throbbing but a single point of light.

Ahead, a gap. A window of inviting darkness. Above, a faded and rotting blue shop sign.

A hand appeared and, reaching, drew me inside.

I wake in darkness, head ringing like a struck bell.

HIGH DOGGER, A THOUSAND AND SEVENTEEN, EXPECTED
GERMAN BIGHT A THOUSAND AND FIFTEEN BY MIDNIGHT
TONIGHT.

The *Shipping Forecast* still loops gently in my ears. And a voice, another voice, cutting through the wash. I turn off the playback and try to tune in.

'And that's not even the best part. Twenty-third of December, wheeling a bike with one flat tyre and carrying a broom in his other hand. Told him we didn't buy books – donations, yeh, sure, sell them back into the community what have you – but when he said it was a clearance, and that the guy had been an artist, I thought again. Asked for his number. He told me his name was Jingle. Winked and said, "Don't tell me it rings a bell". Twenty-third of December, pull the other one, I said, "It's got bells on . . ."'

The voice trails off, gasping, into manic laughter. I try to sit up and open my eyes, but I feel tender and permeable. I lie back down.

'I called. Maybe Christmas had one more miracle? It seemed possible. Original letters by Hemingway, written from Spain. A load of twentieth-century firsts, good publishers, some association copies. Clearly didn't realise what he had, couldn't even find the letters when I went to look at the place, which wasn't his, but had belonged to a friend. A champion ballroom dancer, apparently, who had become a reclusive artist, painting terracotta tiles. Too good to resist. Fuck knows how they met but that was Hackney, I guess. Three-storey townhouse, every surface covered. Made me feel like the place might come down any second. Tried to sell me those first, the tiles; asked if I knew any gallerists who might be interested. But when eventually he did find the letters, in among some stuff about the probate, and I made my offer, he got cold feet. Always happened that way. Could never figure it out. Offer too low and you felt like an arsehole. Too high and they'd think something better would come along.'

None of this means anything to me but the shape it takes, the strangeness of it, makes me wonder if, up until this moment, I have been dreaming. My head is still hammering and my tongue feels unfamiliar. Too large. I wonder if the voice is talking to me, or for its own benefit.

I force myself to sit up and face the voice. A man, wearing a filthy suit, white with blue stripes, and an orange beanie at a jaunty angle. He looks to be in his late thirties. Perhaps the reason that he has stopped talking is that he expects me to say something.

'So, what happened?' I ask, wincing with incipient regret before the words are even out.

'I could go and look, I suppose. It's not far. But I won't. People only want things that are useful.' He spat the last word with contempt.

Images present themselves. The storm, the pain, the hand inside the window of inviting darkness. Words that escaped me are now returning. One word – aphasia – dances limpid and luminous in my mind's eye. A word that describes its own disappearance: the name for the short-circuiting which causes some migraineurs to temporarily lose all of their language, one of those arcane-sounding terms with ancient Greek etymologies with which everyone has been attempting to encircle this newly encroaching strangeness.

A trace of the attack's linguistic fragmentation remains in this luminosity, in a heightened awareness of language's utter artificiality, of the secret life of things beyond it that words can never touch. Not the words themselves, which have been hollowed out to the point of absurdity, but the rhythms of the speaker's voice. Waves lapping against the inside of my skull.

The man struggles to his feet and crosses the room. He starts rummaging through a pile, too indistinct to make out in the gloom, then peers between the cracks in the storm shutters, the light falling across his face. 'I've got a theory. If there was a nuclear explosion tomorrow. If there was a tsunami. If there was an earthquake that split the city in two. Those guys would still be out the front here hawking stolen bike lights.'

Out of the dismantling of the migraine, all of its disfiguring effects, a certainty has been resolving. One that arises out of that secret life below my fragmented language. I need to get to you. I need to share with you, what we now share. Make it a point of . . . something. Connection. Reconciliation. Grounds for understanding and forgiveness. All while I am still tender, still unreconciled to what it is and what it means.

I stagger to my feet, shielding my eyes against the fingers of light wrapping around the ramshackle storm shutters protecting the windows. I want to get out there, be carried by this vibe all the way to Vauxhall, where I hope I will still find you. But the hot blood that rushes to my temples as I stand has different plans. Perhaps a few more minutes rest, before I try my eyes against the sun. I slump back down.

'Have they always been there, then? The hawkers?' I had seen them, bric-a-brac gathered on blankets pulled tight over the cracked pavement. I thought they were a wind-blown recent addition. Perhaps pilgrims, like the ones I'd heard about at St Paul's.

'As long as I have, at least,' he says. I never noticed them, before the Freeze. But there was so much I didn't notice. 'There used to be a guy who would poke his head in, once maybe every eighteen months, to try and sell pillows. Still in their wrapping. Where do these people come from and where do they go? I bet if you dug down far enough, down through the tarmac, the Victorian sewer, the compressed bones of the plague victims, you'd find smashed oil lanterns and rotting sandal straps in the ground below the Kingsland Waste. Buckled chariot wheels.' He starts rubbing his face, scratching his head maniacally, before throwing up his hands. 'What's wrong with you, anyway? Is it really that bad?'

I lean back and catch my balance on something soft. Paperbacks, a huge stack of them, stretching away into the darkness. Behind the wobbling stacks: shelves. More books than I had seen in years.

There is still a certain latency to my thoughts. 'Is this . . . was this a bookshop?'

The man picks up a book in each hand and throws them at me, overarm. I raise my arms, instinctively, to protect my face, but he misses by a good distance. They skid away into the darkness.

A deflated silence, the kind where an incipient threat of violence passes into absurdity.

'I'm sorry,' the man says with a sigh. 'I always get this way, after a migraine. Mood swings. Excitable, euphoric even. Then I have to piss. A huge amount. Then I get depressed.' He casts his arms wide, gesturing at the shelves behind him, at the books covering his legs. 'Yes. It was a bookshop. Obviously it was a bookshop.'

I pick up a book from the pile nearest me to take a look at it. *Critical Research Approaches: New Pathways.* It had a green cover. Below it are ten copies of *Normal People.*

'Don't know what to do with them all,' he says. 'At first, it was just stopping people from burning them for fuel. Simple. Something to focus on. To stick around for. But now . . .' He trails off. 'I keep breaking into abandoned houses, hauling them back here. And at this point, I've really no idea why.' Again, he seems to lose momentum. He starts absent-mindedly gathering up the books around him and returning them to their piles. His movements are automatic. There is something touching in their fastidiousness.

I feel an urge to pacify him. Not out of fear of violence. He has a careworn innocence.

'A friend of mine,' I say, 'we used to go back again and again to the same houses. Once all the food was gone we started collecting other things. Once you pop, it's hard to stop, is all I'm saying.' My voice fades away as I wake up to my disinhibition. 'Is it always like this?'

He is standing over me, a quizzical look on his face. A realisation blooms as a smile. 'It was your first, wasn't it?'

'You got me,' I say.

'How strange, immune since the Thaw and you suddenly develop one now ...' He stretches out his hand. 'Let's start again. I'm Sam.'

I sigh. 'Ellis. I'm Ellis.' I take his hand, and he pulls me to my feet.

Last night's migraine attack was my first. The first of my own. But it wasn't the first I have experienced. That was one of yours.

It's amazing how quickly this has come to seem utterly normal, to live a life where so many firsts are experienced second hand. How quickly the Neurals have come to seem an everyday part of our lives. I don't remember us ever talking about this, but did you know that the technology that has made this all possible was initially developed to help rehabilitate stroke victims? A tiny, subdermal chip planted in the neck, just below the curve of the jaw, sending electrical pulses up the vagus nerve in order to stimulate the brain to reroute brain activity, to open new pathways to replace those that had burned out. It was intended to help those who had lost the use of their legs or had been rendered mute to walk again, talk again.

They just tweaked it, in response to our change in circumstances. It was an easy leap to make, for tech companies looking for new revenue streams: repurposing the chip for data collection and broadcast. Taking something for people who were locked inside their bodies and repurposing it for those forced inside their homes.

An implant that stimulated the brain directly, augmenting reality, it offered retinal projection and haptic feedback. Finally, you could really *see* what others had seen, *feel* what others had felt. One injection, and your nerves were networked into those of countless other people. Not only could you experience other people's lives, you could also offer up approximations of your own experiences, beamed into distant people's bodies.

The implants arrived just as the snow began to fall – with the aid centres, offered for free. Seeing that the economic balance had tipped away from the Global North, a calculation was made. Companies figured that we could still be productive while we sheltered in place.

It was a Faustian pact. We became labourers, mining our sensations. Our lives abstracted out into data points to refine the algorithms that we still hoped would be our deliverance. If we couldn't think our way out this catastrophe, perhaps an intelligence trained on the culmination of our collective experiences might.

It is a promise that still has not delivered. Most of us who could see the exchange for what it was still took the bargain. I wonder if you hesitated, and if so, for how long. Another thing I never asked. Its reach and effects are so much a part of how I've come to know you – it never occurred to me to.

We were all wedded to the idea of work; charity was

something that we bestowed, not received. It was a strange act of mercy, to be allowed to continue in the delusion that we had something to offer.

It wasn't all we got in return. We were saved from boredom, from loneliness. In the darkness of those years when we all thought that the snow would never stop, the illusory connection that they offered was preferable to the total isolation that seemed the only alternative.

After the Thaw, you were one of the first to isolate the migraine aura. Not just the images – the hovering lights – but also all of the other sense data: the strobing sensations, the animated sense of disorder. You were also one of the first to take and arrange it into a clip. Something that could be shared, replicated, altered, modulated. An aurashow.

Yours was one of the first I saw, felt, experienced.

When so many people were struck down by them, I was pleased that I didn't suffer from migraines, that I was one of the very few that had been spared. It felt like one bright spot of good fortune after a run of bad luck.

But soon enough, it was all anyone wanted to talk about.

I was lying on my bed, when I came across one of yours. The first thing, in your aurashow, was a sense of dread. A large shape lifting the hem of a still lake. I now know that this is consistent with the real thing. The anticipation. Time thickening.

But for a few seconds after I began the playback, it seemed as though nothing else had changed. The usual glimmer of visual dissolution, as my brain tried to reconcile the real world – or the one my eyes perceived – with the one being interposed by the implant, didn't occur.

Then, a wobble. The edge of the curtain seemed to lose

confidence in the definition offered by the sun. It warped outwards, before curling back on itself: a snail's shell of fabric with a lacuna made of light at its centre.

Up to this point I had always been able to hold the world and the implant's augmentations apart: to see the real through the gauze of fictive images. It had never occurred to me that the distinction might blur. But now, as the edges began to bleed into one another, I gained a glint of awareness of what this unquestioned confidence had meant.

Instinct made me turn my head towards this glitch, to take hold of it by bringing it to the centre. But as I turned, the wobble shifted.

It was planted in my peripheries. I blinked. The snail had been joined by another, and another. They were on the march. I turned my head left and right and they fed on whatever my eyes lighted upon. Snails made of desk. Snails made of lamp. They were like pearls of windblown rainwater migrating over the glass of the world. Still, I pursued the hole at the heart of each, in turn. The absence made of light.

The snails began to collide and unfurl into a cascade of pearlescent lightning, drawing the fabric of the room into its arc.

As suddenly as it had started, it ended. The room reassembled itself.

There was no sense of you, in this. No sense of the sickness and pain that would come after this slow-motion firework display. But I glimpsed something in that lacuna. Something that called to me at the bottom of the hole at the heart.

I played it again, and again.

There were many theories, in the early days after the Thaw,

as to why the headaches had started. Everything was contested. It was the logical endpoint of the fragmentation that began long before the Freeze, with every person searching for their own truth and abandoning a common one.

The first assumption was that the Neurals were to blame. Overstimulated frontal cortexes. But the problem was general, not confined to those who had offered up their brainstems. Electrical storms thundered across the grey matter of those that remained unaugmented, too.

But it was the weather. All along, it was the weather. After the snow melted, it became more and more unpredictable, and the headaches became more frequent and acute. The weather changed, and people got migraines. The correlation should have been impossible to contest, had people not long ago lost faith in simple cause and effect.

As we all fell into the patterns of this new life, its pace and rhythms dictated by the extreme atmospheric pressure changes and the brain weather that it produced, all the content pipelines we had developed lost their appeal. Representation had already reached a point of crisis, even before the Freeze, because of the rate at which an occurrence was metabolised by the feeds. If a turtle riding the back of a capybara was caught on camera in the morning, it had its own social accounts by lunch and by the time the sun set in Brazil it rose in China over factories printing T-shirts and fidget spinners with their likeness. Every occurrence was evacuated of meaning so quickly that it was barely over before it became a meme for something else.

Now, reality became interesting again, in all its grub and grain, which revealed that reality content – with its grotesque and cartoonish enlargements and exaggerations – had become so untethered that the only reality it could lay claim to was its own: glass-eyed, silicone and alienating. An advert for itself.

Everyone was bored by this, so what happened next was, I suppose, the obvious thing. The oldest thing. The first thing. People started making art from life again.

At least, people like you did. People with migraines. Or, more specifically, those with aura – that neurological tectonic foreshadowing that produced the kinds of visions that in other times had seen people proclaimed mystics or burned at the stake. Although the vast majority of the population had succumbed to the changes in neurological climate, some remained immune. Like me.

But not you. Your pain had made you famous.

Events proliferate. Over the last five years they've increased at such a rate that they have fallen out of order. Everything is significant, nothing is clear. Whatever happened to one fucking thing after another? Was it really so bad? I'm writing this to find out. If I can pinpoint the exact moment where things went wrong between us, then I might be able to walk that line back.

This is an apology, a prayer. An attempt to set things in order, in order to set them right.

Out in front of the bookshop, the flat light of aftermath. Of high clouds and spent pressure. I breathe in deeply, scouring my lungs with the still-humid air.

'What you have to understand,' Sam is saying, 'is that we were individuals. We had a mania for it.'

'Mmhmm.'

He turns back to the shop, his arm raised aloft, like a ringmaster.

'This bookshop is a monument to our mania. Our insistence that we were individuals. Know what I mean?'

Across from where I stand, there is a midrise block of flats facing Kingsland Road. A number of people loiter in their open doorways, hands rubbing at their eyes or arms raised slantways, shielding their sight from the sun as they take in the scene. It feels novel, and not entirely unpleasant, to be part of this emergence, swimming with the current, part of the general run of things.

'Damn,' I say. 'That's crazy.'

I realise now that you were right. I had fundamentally misunderstood what a migraine is. What it does.

The headache is the least of it, only the most explicable part. And the hallucinations: they are themselves a cipher for a shift in perception, the visual aspect of a much deeper disturbance. The ripples on a mirror lake as tectonic plates crash against one another, inscrutable and unfathomed, miles below.

Right now, I'm in no state to set anything right. I press my eyes closed. Sparks dance white against the pink curtain of my blood. Wild affective states are common in the days after storms, the final part of a migraine episode. As a consequence, I usually stay inside as much as possible.

I want quiet and stillness, to figure out whether this new cleft in the world, starting from a white-hot point at my right temple, holds any other revelations. Specifically, anything that might guide me back to you.

Keeping my eyes closed, in the presence of this stranger, I begin to play back what the chip recorded of the sensations of the previous night. The approximation of the pain is way off the mark – a fly's buzz next to a lion's roar – but the angular spots of light, cascading in from the right side of this storm-darkened vision of yesterday's Kingsland Road, land in my gut like the chorus of a song: one played at the apex of a night out when you're rushing; the chorus of a song that had never *got* you before, but which, cloaked in the projected glow of a chemically augmented fraternal love, will forever jolt you with an aftershock of this new understanding.

It had been horrific. One part of me remembers that. So where did this urge come from, to pick at the scab?

There is an encroaching warmth, caressing my cheek. A faint smell of boiled sweets. I open one eye to find Sam's face almost touching mine. Sunlight catching the point where the dark, twisted hair of his eyebrow lightened to down.

'We need to talk about depersonalisation,' he says.

'What do you mean?'

'I mean, how do you feel?'

'I feel . . . fine. A little spaced out.'

'Do you feel like yourself?'

'Who else?' I say, laughing, a little self-conscious. 'Who else might I feel like?'

Sam narrows his eyes at me, pulling away slightly. 'It's why I refused to get one of those . . . things.' He spits the last word. 'Bad enough, the way that the migraine shakes you out of yourself, but then to further self-alienate by allowing one of those things into your brain . . . it's madness.'

'Don't you get bored?'

'That's one thing books always kept me safe from, boredom. Poverty, not so much. But then you can't have everything.'

'How is that any different, really, from having people's experiences beamed straight into my head?'

'Why don't you try reading one? You might find out,' he says, turning back and disappearing into the gloom of the shop.

I do read, always have, but I've learned that it is always safer to play to expectations, unless there is something to be gained by exposing yourself and subverting them.

I think of the doomed attempts to try and incorporate literary tropes into the metadata I wrote for your aurashows. I thought it might bring some structure, this old technology – something to slow the death spiral into infinite reflexivity.

Your more straightforward approach towards intertextuality was much more effective: superimposing your hallucinations over footage from the moon landings, or from NASA's Curiosity Rover, the last of the national space missions before corporate moved in and took the data private, monetising it by rolling it out on the feeds. With a name like Luna, it was an obvious direction.

One of my favourites, one of the most popular, used the footage of Alan Shepard hitting a golf ball on the surface of the moon. Your star drift of hallucinations sliding in from the top right-hand side of the frame, their scintillating panes refracting and warping the grain of the old footage. In the metadata, I reimagined the conversation between Shepard and the other astronaut.

Fore!

Looked like a slice to me.

That will still be hurtling through space thousands of years after you die.

Way to bring the mood down.

I just wanna tell you how I'm feeling . . .

Throughout the course of the conversation, Shepard morphed into Rick Astley and the chorus of 'Never Gonna Give You Up' came in under their conversation, gradually rising in volume. By the end, both astronauts were shaking their hips to the song, Shepard/Astley waving the club in the air, a parody of a deepfake in deep space.

We tried a version where the dialogue cascaded down the left side of the frame, but it didn't get enough impressions. We pulled it after ten minutes before it could flatline and disappear completely and reuploaded the clean version. It flew. You could only stray so far from the familiar and still get traction. Even your perfectly formed aura couldn't get people to read.

Shepard's transformation into Astley didn't make much sense without the text, but that didn't matter. People understood what he represented. He was a meme, one of the oldest. He brought sense with him. Enough of it that made sense of the rest of the show. The feeds went wild for it.

Still, all of collaboration is a poor substitute for what we would share now.

Sam re-emerges from the bookshop, holding a couple of books in his hand; he holds one of them out to me. But before he can speak I cut him off:

'Look, thanks for pulling me in off the street and everything, perhaps I'll see you around?'

'We're in this one,' he says, ignoring my attempts to pull away. I glance at the battered paperback, a book by Iain Sinclair. 'The bookshop. Walks straight past it in the opening. Very grounding to see yourself portrayed this way.'

I watch the people outside their flats, watching us. The muggy benevolence I had felt wrapped up in has evaporated, their presence now somehow sinister. I want to disentangle myself from this man and be on my way, but a sense of gratitude prevents me from turning to outright rudeness, which I can see is rapidly becoming the only means of escape.

'I won't take it with me now, thanks all the same.'

He sighs, leaning back against his makeshift shutters. 'Can't bloody give 'em away. Tell me. What was your worst job?'

'What's that got to do with anything?'

'Always been one of my favourite questions. Better than "what do you do" – a question that is utterly redundant now, since pretty much everyone is bone idle. You can tell a lot about people by the terrible jobs that they've worked.'

I've spent a lot of time ruminating on things I miss, but bullshit jobs aren't one of them. The first one that comes to mind is working hospitality at a football ground, where someone hung an overcoat over a tray of champagne I held. There's the evening I spent serving vodka slushies at a vacuum-cleaner convention, or the one spent serving crêpes from a tricycle in a burlesque club. Silver service wearing white gloves in the Grand Masonic Lodge. A breakfast service at Lord's cricket ground, where a man shouted at me for serving his coffee before his eggs.

'I think the worst one was a temporary job at Wembley Stadium. Five nights of Take That. Five nights of Gary Barlow delivering the same jokes. Serving beer out of a bag.'

'I'd have taken you on.'

'Sorry?'

'Given you a job. Had a policy. Would never hire people who hadn't worked a shit job before turning twenty. You seem ... capable.'

'Thanks, I guess.' He still holds the book limply in hand, slightly outstretched. 'Perhaps I'll give that book a go after all.'

But as I reach out, he snatches it back. 'Once bitten, twice shy.'

'What?'

'One in the hand is worth two in the bush.'

I initiate my implant and begin to record, coming alive to the idea that perhaps there's something in this play of words that you might find funny. But his mood has changed again.

'Idioms,' he says, deflated. 'Boot-worn flagstones. Beaten

24

earth.' He pauses and steadies himself against the shelf. 'I'm sorry, I'm out of practice at this.'

'This?'

'Yes, this.' He made a vague, wide gesture.

Following the arc described by his arm my eyes alight on the tattered remains of a bus shelter; the red plastic of the lollypop is strikingly unblemished. The city's geography, outside of my running circuits, is still mapped in my head by the old bus routes. It would have been the 149 towards London Bridge and then the 344 to Vauxhall. I close my eyes and ride the bus in my mind: the gentle blur of the city. I'd have been at your doorstep in less than an hour.

This is the strangeness of the city we live in. There is no simple before and after. The Freeze was a period of suspended time and Thaw brought this tentative, uncanny normality.

I feel that more than ever this morning. The fragility of things. The migraine was nerve shattering but now, afterwards things seem, for the first time in a long time, simple. I haven't felt this need for you since our early days together. The days when I felt your absence as strongly as your presence.

'Where are you headed?' Sam asks. I open my eyes, take a deep breath.

'I'm going to Vauxhall, to find someone.' In the light, I'm able to see how dirty I've got, passed out on the floor. I brush myself off.

'This someone, left you?'

I look at him blankly and he holds up his hands, in apology. Or perhaps in defence, it is hard to tell.

'Things are different, now. I'm going to get her back.' Why am I telling him this? Saying it aloud makes me feel ridiculous.

Would I always feel this way, after? Fragile and unboundaried. Prone to sharing details of my life that I would normally labour to preserve even from myself.

'How very exciting. Sounds like a quest. An adventure, even. I wasn't being entirely honest about the boredom. If you're headed that way,' he says, as I make my way towards the door. 'Do you mind if I tag along?'

If I'm going to find my way back to you it makes sense to go right back to the beginning. To when we first met.

You were a pioneer, one of the first to transform the symptoms of migraine into a new visual language. I was a man who spent his days sieving compost and running laps of Hackney in scavenged trainers. It's hardly surprising that I noticed you before you noticed me.

I came across that first aurashow of yours lying on my bed, doomscrolling until my eyes were paper dry one morning, willing myself to start the day. But it wasn't until a few weeks later, and another clip, where the point of view flipped for the final two seconds, close on your face, that I recognised you.

I recognised you but couldn't place you. But then I started seeing you around, mostly when I was running in the morning.

We progressed from nods to cautious smiles to hi, how are yous. Eventually this progressed to pleasantries, to those careful surface-level platitudes that we'd all been relearning since the Thaw.

I still remember the texture of these interactions, the slow dawning of a heightened sensitivity. The words themselves were incidental, an ornament to the fold of your wrist, the dip of your chin as you spoke. This, too, was new. I was slow to clock it. It took months – and a number of these otherwise inconsequential exchanges – for my glaciated mind to respond to the heat of my body.

I had begun to time my runs in the hope that we might bump into one another. I wonder whether you were doing the same, with your walks?

It was a storm that finally brought us together in a way that stuck. The humidity had been cloying all morning. I was waiting for it to lift but after lunch, I couldn't wait any longer. I went out for a run, but I couldn't find my rhythm. The pavements were full of distracted, irritable people – cutting me up and then snapping at me.

The pattern was already becoming familiar to me. By the time I turned onto Dalston Lane, a huge bank of cloud was building in the east. I stopped, shielding my eyes from the glare and taking stock. I briefly considered running back the way I had come, doing a reverse loop, perhaps running across Victoria Park so that I could let the rain wash over me when the storm did break.

People began to stop, raising their faces to the heavens. One woman was opening her eyes wide and squeezing them shut, holding her hands out in front of her in amazement, as though it was the first time she had ever seen them. I headed towards the square, when ten yards ahead of me a man sat down on the pavement, cradling his head in his hands. From behind me, I heard retching and, as I turned, the woman who had been fascinated by her hands began hurling rainbow-coloured vomit over the shoes of an older man who was running past her.

I felt the first stirrings of wind, cutting through the thick air. Rolling thunder in the distance and the hairs on my arms standing to attention at the precipitous drop in temperature. It was going to be a big one.

I decided I would wait it out at the farm. Ever since the migraines started people had become careless, downing tools and scarpering home at the first hint of an attack. And these storms – the big ones – were no joke. Hail stones the size of golf balls. They could come on in the space of moments and the topography of the city made them even more unpredictable. The streets below the rows of tower blocks in Hoxton had been transformed into wind-ravaged ravines, scarred by the impact of wheelie bins, picked up and tossed along by storms like empty tin cans.

As I reached Dalston Square the wind rippled a filthy deck chair, making the canvas twist and snap, then dragging it along the ground. The old library, on the corner of the square, had become the compost and potting shed. A garden fork had been left propped against the wall by the double doors, ready to be picked up by the wind and launched through the plate glass windows. I was continually baffled by the speed at which the hard-won resilience of the people around me, cultivated through the years of the Freeze, evaporated at the first sign of a headache.

Of course there were attempts to track these storms, to predict their emergence. But ever since the gulf stream had dropped, with all of the knock-on effects out over the Pacific, none of the models worked any more. Until new patterns could be identified, until the climate settled sufficiently to create new models, it was pretty hopeless. Without this shorthand, no amount of processing power could make sense of the cascading complexity of the constantly shifting weather systems.

And besides, people like you, those who suffered from migraines, lost all interest anyway. You knew when one was coming, felt it in your bones.

I muttered to myself as I scooped up the fork. Drops of rain the size of saucers were spreading a darkening impasto on the cracked tarmac. The wind was keening through the gaps in the scaffold boards as I pulled the doors shut behind me. They were well fitted, and I could almost hear my blood rattling in my skull in the sudden hush as I felt my way down the corridor towards a room that we used as a compost store. Sighing, I sank down onto my haunches, letting the fork clatter to the ground.

'Ellis?'

I jumped to my feet and span, trying to locate the sound, my eyes still adjusting and hot blood still ringing in my ears. Out of the corner of my eye, I sensed movement. I looked, and there you were.

You shuffled a little, levering yourself upright and pulling your woolly hat down over your ears. I moved towards you, guiding myself with my hands in the gloom and sat down a little distance away. You stared at me with a glazed expression, rubbing the balls of your hands into your temples.

'Luna? Is that you?'

You groaned softly, rocking back against the wall, your head angled up to the ceiling, eyes closed.

The rain was now really falling. We were both silent, listening to its steadily increasing intensity. I still felt a sense of peace when a storm hit, the hammering of the rain: the feeling of it striking your skull. The quilted years of the Freeze were still fresh in my mind, when every sound was buffed of its edges by the powder which gave life an ever-muted sense of claustrophobia, which made you want to scream just to hear the raw of yourself, spittle and burning throat.

Your breathing steadied. I was caught between competing desires to remain in this peace and to speak before it somehow became too awkward. I had that feeling, one I hadn't felt in many years: the one I felt when I ran into someone on the bus or Tube and I'd perform some internal calculation about whether to strike up a conversation, groping for banalities while I felt the moments slipping away, until the point was reached when it was already too late.

'I feel sick,' you said.

What were you doing there? I was so caught up in my own excruciating awkwardness at the time that I didn't think to ask. But now that I come to think of it, I suppose there is a small chance you were there looking for me.

I stood and shifted some compost bags around into a nest. 'Here,' I said, gesturing towards it. You half-staggered, half crawled over to it. 'I saw your aurashow,' I continued, pausing, to see if you would respond. I'd never been brave enough, in our brief conversations, to admit that I had recognised you from the off. But it was clear that we would be here a while, until the storm passed. 'The one with the sun. And the breathing.'

You groaned again.

I thought of the clip in which you first revealed your face. The visuals were a time-lapse thing, the sun – represented by a soft orange orb – arcing across the field of view from left to right, filtered through what appeared to be a wet flannel. There was a light stippling of scotoma – the characteristic migraine visual hallucination – in the top-left, like the spots on an egg. Heavy breathing, heart thudding on the audio. A strobing tingling in the left pinkie from the haptics. Then the point of view flipped for the final two seconds, close on your face, overlaid with a filter with floppy bunny ears and a bandage. Sickbed chic.

'A wet flannel,' you said. 'I had a wet flannel across my eyes. I want a wet flannel.'

I crossed the room to the hand sink in the corner, fishing around in a box for a rag. I ran it under the tap and wrung it out.

'What are you seeing now?' I asked as you raised your head. I sat down next to you and held out the rag. You immediately took it from me, unrolled it and placed it over your entire face.

'Lights. Dots.'

'Like the spots on an egg. Or islands, seen from space?' I suggested.

'Yes, that's it. That's exactly it.' You tried to sit up, to turn to face me, but only got halfway before you gasped and lay back down.

'And how do you feel?'

'Like I want to die. Or throw up.' You pressed the flannel into your eyes with your fingers. 'Like I want to be left alone. Like I want you to . . .' You hesitated. 'Keep talking. Keep describing what you saw.'

You inched closer to me and nestled into the crook of my arm. And that's how it started. With a story. I described the glowing orange orb. I described the sound of your heart in my ears, the coppery taste of your pain in my mouth. When I stopped, you pinched the underside of my thigh and made a small growling sound.

Clearly I was preoccupied with beginnings. So, falteringly, I began to tell you a story about the origin of the archipelago of islands that populated the left-hand side of your vision. About how your eye was earth and how one day, a fisherman deity, floating on its surface, got his hook stuck under a rock at the bottom of your eye's milky sea.

He pulled and pulled, causing pain to arc across the mantle of the earth. He pulled and pulled so hard that the rock came free, and floated to the surface, forming an island. When his hook came up empty he grew frustrated and dropped his line once more. But he was plain out of luck; his hook got stuck under another rock. He pulled and pulled . . . Your breathing steadied. I could feel the gentle rise and fall of your chest against my thigh. I tried to search the feeds, to figure out which archipelago of islands' origin myth I had just appropriated and misremembered. No connection, feeds were dead. Too much atmospheric interference.

Once you fell asleep, I rolled you sideways onto a bag of compost and climbed the two flights to the large room, at the back of the building, that had housed the Hackney Archive. It was an assemblage of artefacts – books, maps, photos, births, deaths – that the library held in collection as an archive of local history. There were zines made by a local community press in the '70s and '80s; a trove of documents about a gin distillery from the eighteenth century located on the River Lee. A patch-work, social history. It had, of course, been ransacked, during the Freeze. The photos caught easily and made good kindling for the books. The collection of Ordnance Survey maps had been pilfered by scavengers who refused to be hampered by the intermittent satellite coverage.

What had survived was the archive of local newspapers. Stored in file boxes, slightly hidden away, they had avoided being made into kindling.

I took some out. The first things that caught my eye were the adverts. I have always liked to read them. As a sat there I built up a picture in my mind of everyday life in a forgotten decade through the products offered by mail-order, services rendered. Dog grooming in the 1980s. Vibrating slimming belts in the 1950s. Cure-all tonics at the turn of the century.

I collected a small hoard and carried them back downstairs, into the gloom. I propped myself up on a compost bag alongside you, enjoying the warmth, the proximity. I had some instinct that surrounding myself in this nest of scraps would say some-thing interesting about me; that they guarded us both from the nakedness of my desire.

But when I woke the next morning in my bed of newspaper, all was quiet and you were straddling me, eating a banana. You broke a piece off and prodded it at my lips until I opened my mouth. You popped it inside, eyeing me with a confusing mix of suspicion and appetite. You squeezed my biceps, as if testing a theory, and then placed your fingertips on my chest.

'Always so hungry, after. Hungry and horny.'

'Good morning,' I said, laughing, uncertain. I marvelled at the ease with which you had closed the distance between us.

My longing for you, for this, had blinded me to the fact that you had wanted me too.

'Did you say my eyeball was the earth?' you said, tossing away the banana skin and beginning to unbutton my trousers.

'You realise you're saying that aloud?' says Sam.

I stop and turn, trying to express impatience with the square-ness of my hips.

'What?'

'Sandalwood. Patchouli. Tobacco. Nutmeg.'

I turn and carry on down the road, throwing up my arms. It's a habit I developed when I moved in with you. Something happened to the algorithm that selected the clips that I was served on the feeds. All of a sudden, I was getting served skincare and outfit-matching tutorials. Self-help stuff on how to fail better and be more present. I became obsessed with trying to fix my profile. I made a list of keywords and, when I was alone in the flat or walking to work, browsing the feeds, I would whisper these keywords under my breath. Masculine scents and language out of the gym lexicon. Barbells. Deadlift. Benchpress. The results were unpredictable. The algorithm didn't know who I was any more and the dissociative drift that came from trying to be more myself, to make myself tangible by describing myself in search terms, really didn't work. It made me feel increasingly – hysterically – separated from the person I was at the start.

But as time has passed, these repetitions have served to empty the words of all meaning. It has become soothing to say them aloud. A kind of mantra.

'Can we take a break?' Sam leans his back against the wall, his bum slowly sliding down until he lands in a thump.

We have travelled barely half a mile, stumbling in a straight line south, down the Kingsland Road, just across the bridge over the now fetid Regent's Canal.

In the years running up to the Freeze, when rents were spiralling and every interesting thing was being pushed to the outer boroughs, the waterways had been the last seam of bohemia. Stitched between the glass high-rises and converted warehouses, carrying their cargo of writers, skaters, graffiti artists, they brought hope to the poisoned brain of the city: rough diamonds in the concrete veins. But after the thaw, the canals never recovered. The locks have been destroyed, the channels silted with detritus released by the melting snow and ice.

'I always liked the boat people,' Sam says, taking in the direction of my gaze. 'Who are the equivalent of boat people, now?'

'The yurt people?'

'The ones in Victoria Park?' He pauses, considering. 'Yeh, I'd say that's pretty accurate.'

'Whenever I went on holiday, before. A little city break or

something, I would always play a game in my head where I would try and map London onto the city I was visiting.'

'I like this game,' he says. 'How about New York? Bushwick was Shoreditch.'

'No, Williamsburg, surely.' I am transported back, for a moment, to another life. A week spent in Brooklyn with an ex-girlfriend. The leaves turning in the park at Fort Greene. Accidentally spending fifty dollars at the salad bar in Whole Foods. 'Bushwick was more like . . . Hackney Wick?' I continue, 'and Fort Greene was Haggerston.' We had imagined parallel lives for ourselves there. I'd be studying political science at Columbia, spending my days in the cavernous reading room of the New York Public Library. She was going to meet Anthony Bourdain on a crowded subway platform and make him laugh (*have you heard the one about the butter? Don't spread it*). He would offer her a job on his show, there and then. It was the beginning of the end of our time together, but we didn't know it then; we were finding a gentle way to break to another – to ourselves – that our lives were headed on different tracks by imagining another life where they diverted, but together. I wonder where she is, now.

Was there a moment like this between you and me? Was I too close to see it? Had we been staggering along this way, even before the betrayal? The betrayal. Betrayed. I'm still calling it that, then, am I? It's the feeling which wells in the pit of my stomach whenever I think about our parting. But it's not really a betrayal, is it? You didn't . . . Not really. The false equivalence is beginning to fray, the feeling in my stomach is beginning to fade, replaced by another, heavier still.

All of this passes over in the time it takes for my eyes to find

Sam's. His pupils contracting. The moment is a little too naked, caught in our own respective reveries.

Three, maybe four bus stops from the bookshop and we're both knackered. I look up to the heavens. Piercingly blue, a colour that I understand as pain somewhere behind my right eyeball. It's a shame; I always enjoyed these mornings after a storm. It's the only time when you feel the benefit of being well.

'I find it hard to imagine you in Bushwick,' I say.

'Yeh, well. I wasn't always this way.'

'True of all of us. We should get T-shirts made,' I say. 'Why *are* you following me, anyway?'

'I stashed something, near Old Street, that I need to collect. It's nice to have the company.'

I'm about to ask what would possess him to store something *there*, when there comes the crackle of a loudspeaker. A muezzin's voice starts up behind us, across the street, projecting from the minaret of the Suleymaniye mosque. Sam closes his eyes, smiling.

'Beautiful,' he says. 'Isn't it.'

I nod, watching men emerging in ones and twos from buildings and side streets, with rolled prayer mats under their arms. The mosque has broadcasted the call to prayer all the way through, the swoop and roll of the muezzin's voice calling back the faithful. I've grown attached to the sound, how it marks the passage of the day. It has been one of the only places of worship continually occupied all the way through the weather, a safe harbour.

It makes me think of Malik. Once a week he would go to eat the grilled chicken served out of a tent erected at the side of the mosque, even though he wasn't religious. I was shy of it, would make him get a portion for me.

I haven't spoken to him since you left. I've blamed him at times. It's the longest we've gone without speaking since ... well, as long as I can remember. I wonder to myself what he would have made of Sam. I don't think he would have thought much to his oblique conversational style.

I suppose I have allowed myself to become a little isolated.

As the voice dies away, the stream flowing towards the mosque thins. Sam scans the faces of the final people to arrive, folding their coats across their stomachs as they rush across the cracked tarmac. He watches the faces of the men who mill together at the entranceway, speaking quietly to one another with their heads bowed in huddled solemnity.

'I'm starting to feel like you're looking for someone, too,' I say.

'Isn't everyone?' he says, with an ironic grin. I follow his gaze and watch; as the men file into the mosque, two others approach. One holds a device in his hand and his companion gestures to it. I recognise the one holding the device but can't place him. Each man they approach shakes his head in turn.

'Those two certainly are.' I wonder if they are among the many who had been drifting back since the Thaw, seeking out loved ones that they had been separated from. Some of the un-successful searchers stuck around but most drifted on. The wall of faded photos at the farm always bothered me. So many faces that people had started sticking them on top of one another. I glance at the man I recognise once more; perhaps it is from those photos that I know his face. But there is a cold, snaking feeling that stops me from saying anything aloud, and makes me want to turn away.

Sam clambers to his feet, turning south. 'OK, I'm ready to move on.'

'Wow. Thought you were a Samaritan.' He walks on without turning. With a sigh, I follow, sarcasm hiding my relief. 'Part time I guess.'

We walk in silence, continuing south. In a few minutes we come alongside the Museum of the Home. Was it you that told me it had been built by a slaver? Almshouses which had been turned into an exhibition of domestic life: a kind of Madame Tussauds of interiors. Whenever I passed, I felt a pang of guilt. Malik and I liked to come and visit together, in the early days, putting on stupid voices and pretending that we were two little Lords. There was a fleeting thrill in crossing the threshold and becoming a part of the furniture.

Do you remember that beautiful Ercol dining set that I wanted to bring to your flat? Over the course of four days, I single-handedly liberated it from the 'living rooms through the years' display. It was when I was carrying the final chair on my back like a tortoise that I heard the sound of an explosion from out in front of the museum. I froze, straining under the weight of the chair, but there was no further sound. Once I recovered my wits, I crept to a first-floor window and peered out.

I immediately located the source of the noise. The walled garden out in front of the almshouses was lined with enormous London plane trees which were now half-buried by the snow and stripped of their leaves by the wind. One of these trees had been reduced to splinters. I couldn't quite understand it, but it seemed to have exploded. Steaming hunks of shattered wood radiated from the ruined trunk. There was no one else in sight.

It was only once I got back to my flat and did some research that I realised that it wasn't vandalism but simply the gradual expansion of the freezing sap that had caused the tree to explode. It felt like a portent, a sign of spectral surveillance.

The ruined husk of the exploded tree is now stripped of its bark and leaning against the boundary wall. All of these memory objects. All of them somehow pointing back to you.

I would have taken more if I had known that the group of Neural refuseniks who were currently camped out there would move in during the Thaw. People like Sam who had stayed behind but chosen not to take the implant. They were hostile, and strange.

Despite my scorn, I have always enjoyed the idea of people who had chosen to become relics moving into a museum of the home. In a way, I'm just like them. I've fashioned a museum out of the whole borough; I'd been tending the displays on my circuits. This newfound clarity makes the place feel suddenly stifling. I'm glad to be on the move.

'Did you ever consider moving in there?' I ask.

'Why? Because I refused an implant?'

'You're following me, you say, for the company. How long have you been living in that empty shop?'

'Not taking an implant doesn't make me like them,' he says. 'They've made a cult of not having one. Which is as bad as having one, in my book.'

I think of my list of search terms. 'Don't all rituals seem a little ridiculous, at first?'

'Everyone is an expert in symbols now. All of you who spend your days pouring them directly into their brainstems from the fucking feeds.'

'Why do they bother you so much?' I ask. I'm now genuinely

curious. His irritation seems excessive; the Neurals are mostly harmless, unlike so much else.

His mouth puckers in surprise as he considers, for a moment. 'Don't you want more?'

'More what?'

'More than some invented shared purpose. More than withdrawing from the world and forgetting that you were a part of it.'

'I never withdrew,' I say. 'I've been here, this whole time.'

'Don't you want to be able to draw a line, backwards in time?' He pauses again, looking for the right words. 'To be continuous?'

Again, this all feels too naked. Because it is exactly what I want. What I've only just realised that I am missing. So of course, I deny it. 'I want to move on.'

Sam stops, suddenly, and turns on his heels. 'Can we turn just up here?' he asks. 'I don't know if you had a route in mind, but this is the quickest way to Old Street.'

An intention has been forming since we had passed the mosque. Last night's migraine attack implied alternate connections, pathways heretofore hidden. I feel frayed and conductive. I want something of the sobriety expressed by the line of the men's necks as they waited for prayer outside of the mosque, bowed by the gravity of grace. If that's what it is. I feel the weight and before I find my way back to you, I need to understand something of its direction.

'OK, but after that I want to go by St Paul's,' I say. 'I've been meaning to go and see a service there.'

My recent isolation makes it difficult to feel my way back to the early days between us.

I do know that my need for you, when it arrived, did so with such force that it overwhelmed me. It surfaced not as an onrush of straightforward desire, but was instead prefigured by a flood of apologies. My feelings were embarrassing in their intensity.

It was so easy to fold our lives into shapes that would tesselate that we did it almost without noticing.

You didn't have to work, at least not in the conventional sense. All the stuff that people sent you. Cut wildflowers. Freeze-dried berries. Weirder, wilder stuff – meant as a comment on, or in compliment to, your work. Buttons mudlarked from the Thames estuary shoreline after waterspouts had dredged them from their resting places, nudged by the tide.

Crumbs of comets. Polished pieces of quartz in jute bags. You piled them in a magpie cache by your door, and if you ran out of any supplies, you would grab something to trade for a bag of apples or a block of tofu.

All of this would arrive by drone. They were one of the first things that enterprising people fabricated after the Thaw – you just needed a 3-D printer and a single-board computer. Delivery co-ops had sprung up, run on a similar principle as the farms. Offer something up, food or labour, and those that had the know-how to build the drones would deliver something in exchange.

Since it had been built, I'd had mixed feelings about the rust-coloured luxury tower block where you lived, opposite Haggerston station. Pre-distressed to clothe itself in the valour of the working-class communities it had displaced, it was one of the only continuously inhabited buildings in the area because of its views over the city and proximity to the distribution centre in the Overground station.

I was quite quickly convinced of its charms and soon I found myself staying up with you through the night. Mostly, we were watching the feeds. You would crop, snippet and repackage old aurashows as a way of linking people back to their original mint. Chuck on a chipmunk filter or tinker with the haptics. People would clip your videos, and splash their own visuals in overlay.

I loved to watch you work at night. You were instinctive and intuitive; your practice (and your illness) had developed in step with the technology. It was a revelation to find how quotidian the process of creation was.

It quite quickly became obvious how differently we were

wired. You could only focus if your attention was split. While you worked, you would endlessly stream episodes of the same few American shows – *Gilmore Girls*, *Parks and Recreation*, *New Girl* – in a window off to one side, muted with the subtitles on. You would mouth along to your favourite lines, your face transforming as you transported yourself. When you were really absorbed in your work, you would let the same episode loop two or three times before bothering to change it.

You would make cups of herbal tea and leave them to cool, just out of reach, until they were totally forgotten. You would get hungry, make a snack, and forget all about your hunger the moment you lay down again.

It was impossible for me to sustain anything, or read anything, in these conditions. But I didn't mind. It was comforting to be caught in the shield of another person's habits.

You had a notebook, a pen clipped to the front cover, which lived down the side of the sofa. Every now and then, you would get up and fetch it, add a word or two, and then squirrel it away again.

Eventually, I had to ask. 'OK, I'll bite.'

'Bite?'

'The notebook.'

'What notebook?'

'What do you write in there.'

You took it out from the sofa. 'This one?' Deadpan.

'Yes, that one.'

'Lists.'

'Lists? Lists of what?'

'Lots of things.' You opened it up and started flicking through it, thoughtfully. 'I have different headings. And each time I think of a new entry, I add it in.' Opening it to the first page, you cleared your throat. 'Here's how it started. "Migraine is: lightning, fog, copper, teeth, static, sulphur, sick, flare, astral, carnal" . . . it goes on.'

You paused, looking at me, and I could tell that you wanted a response but I couldn't tell what. 'And then, of course, there's "Migraine is not: fair, plans, rain, plastic, window, stillness, blood, time's flow, wave breaking . . ."'

'Is it . . . for your work?'

'I suppose so. More for my amusement. I got the idea from a book. A woman in the Japanese Imperial Court would write these lists, for herself and her friends. Just everyday things. I just felt an urge, to name it, I don't know . . .'

'A journaling girlie.'

'Oh, fuck you,' you said, laughing and stuffing it back down the side of the sofa.

One night, when you had mouthed the same line from the same episode of *Gilmore Girls* for the third time in three hours, you did it with such unconscious seriousness that a fist of feeling pushed itself from my chest up to my throat in a kind of startled laugh.

'If this is boring you,' you said, a shock of hurt creasing your forehead. 'You can change it to something else, you know.'

'I'm sorry, I'm sorry.'

'I don't always watch this stuff. I have seen *The Sopranos*.'

'I'm not laughing at you.'

You glared at me.

'Really I'm not'.

Lying next to you I used my implant to comb the feeds for material that I might contribute to your work – offerings of my own to leave at your door.

Initially, my participation was commentary, making memes out of stills from your aurashows and posting them below clips generated by other migraineurs. But then I set out to find material to augment the work itself, plundering any digitised archive that had survived the chaotic rupture of the last ten years to find primary material that everyone else, shepherded algorithmically through their days, had been gliding straight past.

Also, on the days I did go back to work at the farm, I started bringing back items from the archive on the third floor of the old library. I would lay them out on your coffee table and leaf through them while watching the weather move over the city.

As your channel was gaining popularity, more and more people were 'reaching out' to offer rewards for you to post sponsored content. Since the weather changed all manner of remedies had sprung up to compete for the attention and resources of the agonised majority, desperate to believe that a new gel, or a new patch, might be the key to freeing their tangled and misfiring nerves.

You had always been reluctant to entertain any offers. Other people were beginning to use their aura to direct people towards cures that spanned the dubious to the outright dangerous: toxic seminars on the power of positive thinking, tinctures concocted from medieval textbooks out of artificially synthesised rosemary and vegetable fat which promised to 'rebalance your humours', lessons in self-trepanning from wild-eyed fanatics with scars whiskering their femoral veins.

You felt a responsibility towards your followers. You didn't want to leverage their shared pain into creature comforts.

I loved the softness of these nights spent together, but by the morning I felt restless, somehow stifled. I would sleep for a few hours and then dress to run around the neighbourhood.

In the dawn light, it felt natural that the streets were deserted, that the houses were dark. The people, like the day, were imminent. I developed a route, a new circuit to haunt my old neighbourhood with new desires. West through de Beauvoir, up the shuttered high street on Southgate Road – where I would sometimes, in the past, buy an overpriced Scotch egg – all the way to Balls Pond Road, a road that was so associated with the 38 bus in my mind that I still half expected one to tear past me at any second.

As I ran I sought out leanness, parachuting myself back into the person that I had been; the fug of domesticity felt dangerously complacent. I had to shed it.

*

The first aurashow that you and I made together came out of an attempt to resist this impulse that I felt while I was running: out of some attempt to reconcile the old and new.

I was avoiding Malik then, too. You know by now he is the only other person who I really care for. It was part of the reason I was leaving the house so early, why I preferred to stay at yours. I had an instinct that whatever was growing between us was too fragile to survive an interrogation.

Over the past few years he and I had become inseparable.

Like me, he was one of the minority who didn't suffer from migraines. He had developed a sideline in pharmaceuticals that he fabricated in one of the abandoned garages under the railway arches near the station. After a few weeks, spending nights at your place, I went to see him. He feigned disinterest, acting as though I hadn't vanished. A protective impulse that we had all developed.

His garage was a cluttered toy shop of machinery, spanning centuries. Malik's dad had run a house-clearance outfit with a special interest in mid-century furniture and a general interest in just about everything else. At school, Malik was always bringing in trinkets he'd pinched off his dad. He had an endless supply of Zippo lighters, engraved with forgotten milestones.

His dad had done well enough for himself that he'd ended up living in Harlow, two doors down from Rod Stewart. He'd left when the Freeze set in. Packed up a load of furniture in his Luton van to barter for his future comfort. He slid off the M20 in a blizzard in the early snowfall, trying to make it to Dover. Malik had stayed and inherited his dad's entrepreneurial kleptomania. The garage was a kind of tribute.

The first few months, after we had decided to stay, had been a frenzy of accumulation. We liberated everything we could and brought it back here. So much of it useless. We existed then, in a doubled state: knowing that everything was changing and hoping that it might go back to the way that it was. If everyone did end up flooding back, we felt we were owed a material advantage. And if it really was the end, we wanted to go out wearing C.P. Company. That's why, in Malik's garage, boxes of unopened trainers were stuffed next to cordless drills and flat-screen TVs.

Over time, I lost interest. Air Max 95s weren't much use in six feet of snow. But the habit of accumulation is hard to kick even when consumption becomes totally inconspicuous.

When I told him about you, about us, he reached into his

bag and brought out what looked like a glue stick, wrapped in a jaunty paper sticker with the word 'PrikStik' printed along the side in bright red and black lettering.

'Bit of Tiger Balm, bit of ibuprofen – tell her to give it a try,' he said with a wink, handing it over to me. He opened his mouth to ask a question but thought better of it. I was grateful to get away.

When I got back to the flat, you gingerly applied some to your right temple to humour me. 'Soothing', was your verdict. 'At the very least it doesn't seem to be full of rat poison.'

But you *did* continue to use it. A few nights later, as you were manipulating clips projected onto your ceiling, I was combing the digital archives to try to find something that might augment your visuals.

Secreted in the catalogue of the Wellcome Collection, I stumbled on a reference to something called the 'Migraine Art Competition'. It had invited sufferers of migraine to submit, by post, artworks which illustrated the hallucinations, pain and general disruption to their lives caused by their migraine attacks.

A little more research revealed that it was sponsored and partially conceived by a marketing executive from a pharmaceutical company who wanted materials to promote a migraine drug. The competition offered the perfect opportunity for market research.

I found the archive. Five hundred and sixty-two entries from the four competitions, scanned in high definition. I flicked through them, a dizzying carousel of crenellated patterns, faces creased in agony, newsprint cut into spirals winding in on themselves, still lives overlaid by miasmatical vapours.

One snagged my attention. I flicked past and then flicked back – a detail made me laugh aloud.

'Hmm?' you said.

'Check this out.'

You had an old projector set up, trained on the ceiling, so we could lie next to one another on cushions and stream the visual and audio from our implants for the other to see. It felt more like a shared experience that way. I cast the image above us.

It showed an androgynous face, garlanded with bouffant, mousy hair, parted to one side. But in the place of facial features was an old-fashioned arcade game machine, complete with joystick and buttons, with 'Migraine Computer' in lit-up letters at the top. The screen's machine showed the classic migraine 'fortification' aura, a circle of illuminated jagged lines, like the ramparts of a castle.

'We could use this,' I said.

It was amazing how quickly the hyper-specific language around migraine presentation had become its own currency. Here, below the screen of the arcade machine, you could choose between the various 'Scotoma' – rainbow, fortification, stellate etc. – the names given in medical parlance to the characteristic shapes that the migraine visual disruptions took.

What had once been set down as an inside joke would now have an outsize audience. As with everything, you were an early adopter. Your tag was @snailstar, an amalgamation of the two shapes most often to be found in your aura.

'We could layer the image, like this,' you said. The image above us phased almost imperceptibly. The static fortification aura shown on the machine's screen disappeared and was replaced with a cosmic drift – the stars of your migraine hallucinations expanding and contracting as they moved from one side of the screen to another.

There had been some attempt by men who didn't suffer from migraine, who argued that they were being persecuted for being in a minority, to weaponise this language against the people who sought to hold it up in self-definition. Voices on the feeds who said they had been forced to adjust their lives to match the rhythms of weather and headaches. But it fell flat.

Most saw which way the wind was blowing and moved with it. In their patched-together labs on ragged industrial estates, freelance pharmacists like Malik had come to the same conclusion as the marketing man who conceived of the Migraine Art Competition: who better to promote a cure than those who suffer most?

I saw an opportunity to help a friend while also having the chance to feel like I was contributing to some of the comforts that you had been, in your offhand and generous way, sharing with me in the few weeks we had been seeing each other. I rolled over, to get your attention, and explained my idea.

I watched a series of emotions and possible responses move over your face under the dim hue of the projector. Then you rolled your shoulders, wrinkled your nose and said, 'Why not, let's do it'. And we set to work.

I messaged Malik to explain and he pinged me back immediately, a message full of exclamation marks and promises for any referrals that came his way.

That night, we transformed the image you had made into an arcade game for the implant: 'choose your blighter!'

The player manipulated the joystick to guide a little

rocket ship through the gradually encroaching hallucinatory formations.

But whichever level was picked, the images would grow and multiply until they filled the field and navigating the ship through them became impossible. When the ship crashed, it exploded. The aura turned blood red and dematerialised, re-forming to make the words: 'game over', with haptics fizzing down the length of the viewer's arms.

The game would be irresistible because migraine itself progressed with the same inevitability as a game of *Space Invaders*. The player could see the catastrophe coming, the gradual encroachment of the aura across the visual field. But in the end, there would be no escape. Pain and darkness would follow.

At this point, your face, the one known on the feeds, pinched and faded by the typical bloodless migraine pallor, floated out of the background. Below your face: 'play again? yes / no'.

Select yes, and a disembodied PrikStik spiralled its way onto the screen, sparkling and shining. Once applied to your temple, your face brightened, blood returning your cheeks, before a beatific smile caught at the corners of your mouth. A halo dropped down from above and your image misted and ascended, as the viewer was returned to the first image, back at the helm of the rocket ship. A chance to play again.

By now, dawn light was spearing through the closed storm shutters and we were both exhausted and giddy. You were working on the cover thumbnail when you called me over.

'Look at this,' you said, enlarging the image on the ceiling until it just showed the side of the arcade machine: a detail which we had so far neglected. In large, black vertical letters was written: 'Supplied by Nature's Rotten Tricks Co.'

The next morning, in a haze of ecstatic exhaustion, we went to a guy I knew from the farm, who used to have a tattoo parlour on Kingsland Road, and traded a packet of goji berries for two identical tattoos.

Nature's Rotten Tricks Co. Our new partnership was inked onto our forearms.

Following Sam along Hoxton Street I feel a newfound affinity with that tiny spaceship. I catch myself muttering my incantation once again. We pass a shop where I once had my bike repaired; a cafe where, one sticky Saturday morning, a girlfriend had broken up with me while I was still ordering a coffee.

I have resisted for as long as possible but, in the shadow of the shell of the art'otel, I check your feed to see if you've posted anything since last night's storm.

The network is back up. One post. Strong haptics. Fingertips abuzz, with the sensation rebounding up the length of my forearms. In the visuals, the aura is abstracted: strobe-like vectors sped up so that they fill the field in a matter of seconds, before dissolving to reveal your face. Mist, halo, ascension. A sequence

I shot in the flat, images pulled from my very own eyeballs. A rehash of old material.

Since you left, I always tell myself that I'll resist, but I've amazed myself with my total lack of resolve after each storm. I want to tell myself that your aurashows are less interesting, but perhaps the fact that you're spending less time on them isn't something I should be encouraged by.

Having finally experienced a migraine for real, the simulation seems flat. The haptics lack gradient, that tidal sense of sensation swelling and receding. The binary activation and deactivation of nerve endings that the implant allows is a more effective metaphor for the mental disorientation – time slipping, in staccato steps, out of joint – than it is for the physical discomfort that it is supposed to simulate.

Already I can feel a curtain drawing over my experience of the previous day. The pain and foggy febrility are the only remnants of the sense of total hijack I felt, stumbling into the bookshop. There's no way to record the violent unravelling of the knot of self. In the wake, there seems to be some psychic safety measure in action, an invisible hand straining on the end of the rope, tightening it back into place. I haven't considered before that I have been surrounded by people who, once every few weeks, forget the trick of being themselves.

I can't remember it, exactly, because memory is part of the trick. So, in the place of a memory, I can feel a black fear forming, cloaked in a primal instinct: to look away.

Maybe I will make this my project, on the feeds. I'll find a way to finally embody depersonalisation.

I watch one more loop of your haloed face ascending before I tune out. Perhaps I should send you a message, to let you know I'm on my way? I try to think of some words to convey this growing understanding I feel in my chest, but nothing seems right. I don't want to fall back into the pattern we had, and summoning anything from the web of associations that we built together would do exactly that. Better that I just turn up.

Sam is waving his fingers in front of my nose. 'Never going to get used to that.'

'Used to what?' I say.

'People disappearing, in front of my eyes.'

He picks up a windfall tomato. The hotel was never finished, there is no glass. On the ground floor, the hoarding still shows, in faded vinyl renderings, what the place was going to look like. Huge beds with hospital corners, chrome fittings and tastefully bland abstractions lining the walls. About three floors up, some of the storm shutters are hanging open. There are tomatoes, mostly unripe, strewn across the floor in front of us.

A less disciplined farm than our one on Dalston Square. A smaller, newer one, probably, this close to the city. The wind has been allowed to blow right through.

'Why did you bring us this way?' I ask.

'Come on,' he says, picking up a tomato and biting into it like an apple. 'Best not hang around.' He starts off in the direction of the roundabout.

All of the shops on Old Street are derelict, windows smashed, not a storm shutter in sight. In front of the old fire station a sapling is growing through the fissured tarmac.

'Had my first bookshop job here, under the roundabout,' Sam says. 'Camden Lock Books. The name confused the hell out of the tourists, but we liked it that way. Selling remainders to the baby-faced tech titans. Google put us on a billboard above the roundabout.'

'I haven't been through here in years. Probably not the best day for it,' I say.

'Seems quiet enough to me.'

When the migraines first started, people returned to comb over offices that had been abandoned during the Freeze. Despite the obvious correlation with the weather, there was an effort to find some evidence that the pain was part of a wider plan. One theory, dominant for a while, was that the migraines were the effect of some inbuilt redundancy in the implants, a deliberate flaw in the design that would require those implanted to upgrade every few years or begin to disintegrate; a kind of digital feudalism where you'd be forced to pay ground rent on your own body to the tech companies who implanted you.

'Did you ever buy into the redundancy theory?' I ask. I'm curious to see whether Sam has fallen prey to the general rejection of simple cause and effect.

He taps his temple. 'Wouldn't explain why a broken sky cleaves me open, too, would it? Doesn't mean that something along those lines *couldn't* happen though, nothing to stop them.'

The theory went that we were all doomed to wait for an upgrade that would now never come.

All of the theories come out of a twisted hope that that there is an insidious force – or in fact, any force – shaping events. But the only real conspiracy is one of blindness, to something so simple – our contingency. Our homeostasis is an expression of the earth's own; as it sickened, so have we.

There are some who have continued to believe it though.

The theory still has a kind of emotional cogency that remains persuasive even after it has become clear that no concrete evidence will ever emerge. People just need someone or something to blame.

The stink of resentment hangs over the place. In the days after storms people wander down here – on their own, or sometimes in groups – to perform a kind of ritualised desecration, to exorcise their pain and rage. So, even as the city has begun to fill up again, as people drift back after the Thaw, they have avoided the roads radiating from the old roundabout. The buildings were gradually stripped and nature, in her steady persistence, has begun to take the area back.

Sam points up at one of the tower blocks, looming behind the fire station.

'One of my best customers lived up there. Gordon. He'd been living in there since they built it. Sixty years. Still think about him all the time.'

'He still there?' I asked.

'I don't know,' Sam says, sighing. 'A professional gambler and a wine broker. Never learned how to use a computer, had a mobile phone he never turned on, and always paid in cash.'

He picks up a lightbulb, shakes it. The filament inside rattles. He throws it back to the floor, continuing: 'Every truly great reader has one true obsession, and his was the Dutch old masters. He went to Amsterdam once for a Vermeer exhibition and went every day, for a week. Whenever I went on holiday somewhere in Europe he'd give me a list of hidden treasures: altarpieces in Parisian churches, paintings hidden in municipal offices in Madrid.'

'A good friend to have. How long had you known him?'

'Must have been fifteen years. He wouldn't have thought of me as a friend though, I don't suppose. You see someone every week. Piece by piece you learn every detail of their lives. What's happening with their doctor. How they dread their granddaughter's calls, her inane questions a constant reminder of how it's all too little, too late. And then one week, you notice they haven't been in for a little while; their uncollected orders are stacking up under the desk. You call them, no one answers, and then another customer comes along and you forget about it again. Until a few months later, when you get a call one day out of the blue: a young woman who found your number on a postcard on her grandad's desk when she was clearing it out – do you want to buy some books? And then they're back on the shelves, each one an episode in a conversation – the chain that it formed carried off, link by link.'

'There was a lot of uncertainty,' I offer. 'Those first few months. There are a lot of people I wonder about.'

Sam is about to ask more, but the question catches in his throat as, five feet in front of us, a microwave sails out of a first-floor office window and crashes onto the pavement. I crouch and my hand goes to my ankle, to the knife I keep strapped there.

A manic laugh floats out in its wake. We wait, stock still, for a few moments but when there is no more movement I gesture silently to the other side of the road and we tiptoe across. We are almost at the roundabout.

'You got down pretty quick, there,' Sam says. I follow his wary eyes to my hand, which makes me realise it still holds the knife. I kneel and put it back into its sheath, clipping it closed.

'First thing you did,' I say. 'Was look over your shoulder. Are you being followed?'

'What on earth are you talking about?' Sam folds his arms.

'Those two men at the mosque?'

'You're paranoid.'

'Can we hurry the fuck up and get this done?' I say. 'What *exactly* is it that we're doing, anyway?'

'Often happens after a migraine. Everything seems connected, a little like psychosis. You should be careful.' He skips ahead, descending the steps into the old Tube station, beckoning me on. 'It will only take a minute.'

'In there?'

'Come on.'

'Is it safe?'

'Aren't you curious?' he says, clicking on a torch. I can hear the self-satisfied lip curl in his words.

Since the Thaw, the Tube network has been flooded. I follow two steps behind. The bottom of the staircase is submerged, the torch's beam reflecting off the black oily surface of the standing water. The meltwater has brought with it illnesses that the city hadn't seen for centuries: cholera, dysentery and polio.

'Are you going in there?' I ask.

'No, no. Just one second.' He pulls at some loose brickwork in the wall of the stairwell, bringing out a number of clear plastic bags and checking them over under the light of the torch.

'Fleet, Westbourne, Tyburn . . .' Sam mutters to himself.

'What are you on about?'

'Rivers,' he says, waving the bags in my face. 'Maps of all the lost rivers of London. My treasure trove.'

'What on earth do you need those for?'

He points at the fetid water at his feet. 'I should have thought the value of them would be pretty clear. Some farmer you are.' He folds them under his arm and sweeps past me, ascending the stairs 'Far safer, here, than at the shop. Where next? St Paul's? You've given me an idea; I have a friend there.'

Here be monsters. Isn't that what they wrote, at the ragged edges of old maps, in the places they were too scared to visit? If I'm going to trace our coming together, to make sense of how we came apart, then it's time to fill in the gaps. The silences. The things we were always too scared to say to one another.

This silence is the spiral. The one that leads away from you.

Did you ever wonder why I was so hesitant to introduce you to Malik?

I need to go further back. You remember what it was like, when the snow started falling, when it felt like everyone was leaving. Those first few months, it seemed like time had suspended, rather than stopped.

And into that suspended time, I roamed with Malik. In the third week, we stole a trolley from the shopping centre and took it over the road to Marks and Spencer, filling it with bottles from the top shelf to push through the snow all the way down the Kingsland Road to Liverpool Street where people were fighting each other to fill the trains to the coast, to the exit point, and we laughed and screamed ourselves brave and warm, rocking a bus until it rolled and fell, a red body chalk outlined by the fresh powder and more snow fell. More people left.

And we followed our ears to a sound system dragged from one of the Dalston basement clubs and danced to keep ourselves warm to disco, to house, to techno, and partnered up and peeled away to fuck standing up in the lee of a bus stop, a camel in a snow suit.

More snow fell, and we walked all the way to Oxford Street, to see the stripped mannequins, standing in the darkened windows. And we walked all the way to Regent's Park, to see the empty cages at the zoo. And we walked to St Katharine Docks to throw bricks at bankers as they escaped in their gilets on their pleasure boats. And we walked to the Tower, to try to spot the last raven take flight. And we walked to the South Bank, to hear our voices echo in the Turbine Hall, to hear our voices echoing out across the river. And we walked to Canary Wharf, to watch planes leaving and arriving until they were only leaving, banking away towards the continent. And we walked to watch the city slow.

Someone grounded a Thames Clipper on the foreshore by London Bridge. Someone stole a fire engine and drove it into the canal. Someone climbed Nelson's column and turned the old goat into a snowman – finished the thing off with a carrot and two pieces of coal. Still the snow fell. Still, people left.

But not us. We walked to Mayfair, to snatch Trojan helmets

off plinths – looted for the hundredth time to nestle on our greasy nests of hair. To dip eight-hundred-pound pairs of trainers in pink paint and walk through the thick pile of a private members club.

And we went into houses and dug out car keys and raced each other through the empty streets until Malik crashed on one of the estates by the Angel and we ran and ran, laughing, as though someone would be coming after us.

And the snow fell until there was no more *as I live and breathe* no more *how's your father* no more nights for the ages and days when time turned in on itself.

And eventually, the snow was too high for trolleys. It was too deep for the Chelsea tractors that had been left abandoned outside the townhouses.

But it wasn't for any of these episodes, themselves, that I have avoided talking about that time, but for what came just after.

It was around then, when our antics were beginning to slow – when we were beginning to grow bored – that it happened.

Memories still intrude, of that day. Never in sequence and never complete. A fallen glove. A lock of black, greasy hair escaping a woollen beanie.

Malik and I had been combing houses at the top of London Fields.

It had been a good day, our bags were full and we were about to call it, but with Malik, it was always just one more house. Just one more. I was climbing out of a ground-floor window when I saw a man in a torn snowsuit approach Malik, twenty feet ahead. I was about to call out, but something stopped me. Something in the careful and erect way he moved across the snow, feet crossing like a dressage horse.

He snatched at the bag and as Malik turned, pulled taut, he struck the man across the face. With the blow, I re-animated, watching myself drop from the ledge and bounding over drifts to where they had come together.

The crowbar we used to pry open sash windows was already in my hand. I struck him once – the weight of metal a sufficient counterweight to my hesitation – and he stiffened before toppling, ponderous, like a felled tree.

This is the image that recurs most often. His straightened form not yet falling but hanging weightless, describing a hypotenuse between the earth and the sky.

He never saw my face; is that why I can't remember his? Only the angle of it, profiled against the snow.

*

Every time you and I touched those first few months, I would be sucked back through time to that moment in the snow, standing by Malik's side. The angle of the falling body against the sky. I had been able to supress the memory, and the shame that it summoned, but in doing so I had supressed every other feeling too.

So, when we came together it was with desperation. We folded around one another, oil raked through water. The feeling faded: a darker shade on the palette of our new intimacy. I never stopped to question what was behind the intensity of feeling, on your part. What you wanted to leave behind you.

I idealised you. There was a part of me that wanted to go back in time, to gain re-entry into the land of foreclosed possibilities. Of coffee shops and low traffic neighbourhoods, council tax and credit card bills, of freedom made sweeter by its restriction. I thought that the ecstatic communion of our bodies was some-how a ticket back to this.

And when that wasn't enough, instead of talking about it, I told stories.

This impulse comes from my mum, I think.

She left about a week after that day in London Fields, to make the trip to the coast with a ragged band of pensioners. I was trying to find a way to explain to her what had happened. Looking back, now, I can see that she read my silence as anger, at her decision to leave. Perhaps, if I had been able to tell her, then, it wouldn't have been so difficult to tell you now.

A few days before she left, we shared a cup of tea at her flat and she told me a story about the last few weeks of her own mum's life.

She had died a year before I was born. Mum had never before mentioned the end of Gran's life. When she became too frail to care for herself, she'd gone into St Joseph's over on Cambridge Heath Road, to be looked after by the nuns. Each day, when Mum left for the night, Gran would say to her, 'See you tomorrow, Viv.' And each morning, when Mum came in, there she'd still be, waiting for her to draw the cur-tains. Waiting to greet the sunshine, the gift that Mum had brought her. Until one morning, she wasn't waiting. The bed was empty, the sheets remade. The hospice had tried to call her, but they had taken down the wrong number; Gran had died in the night.

'It wasn't until later that day, when I got home, that I realised what she had said to me the previous night when I left her. I was sat right here. Cup of tea fell right out of my hand, spilled all over the lino. Sobbing like a fool. Every night it had been "See

68

you tomorrow, Viv". That night, when I leaned in, to give her a kiss, it was "Be good, Viv."'

'So . . . she knew, then?'

'Suppose that she did.'

There was a long pause, then. Me willing her not to take the conversation along the track it had started on. 'Anyway,' she finally said, blowing out her cheeks, 'what I'm getting at—'

'Don't,' I interrupted. 'This is a bit bloody morbid for my tastes.'

'All I'm saying is, this is see you later.'

'Bit bloody morbid.'

'Just remember: see you later. Never "be good".' In the absence of anything else to say, she put her hand over mine.

'Fat chance of that in any case,' I said.

She smiled, sad, patting my balled fists. 'And if you can't be good?'

I tried to pull away, physically, from the formula response. She squeezed my knuckles, widening her eyes to flatten the laugh lines.

She said it again, the strain of squeezing my fist entering her voice. 'And if you can't be good?'

I relented. 'If you can't be good, be lucky.'

It's been four years now, since I last heard from her. During the day, I can picture her face. I see it in reflections of darkened shop windows, in the puddles skirting the railway arches, her wry smile framed by the passing clouds. But it's only in my dreams that I can hear her voice. The cigarette smoke of her laugh.

This is the city we live in: a city of disappearances. Of incomplete histories, interrupted, and only partially disclosed.

Recently, on a run through the neighbourhood, punishing my body to pull focus from my thoughts, I passed the spot where the body fell. Forest Road, a line of shattered Georgian houses. I felt a jolt, not of sadness but rather desire.

I understand now that there was always this transmutation at play, between you and me – an attempt to live with our feelings by turning them into something else.

This is why we had to hold each other at arm's length. Why we had to tell ourselves stories about each other, to ourselves. An attempt to find another route to the understanding that our bodies found so easily.

A few weeks after we met, I came up with this story for you about a woman who wakes from a storm to find out that her life has changed. I told it one night, lying on the floor of your flat, lit by the glow of the feeds projected onto the ceiling.

The change in this woman's life wasn't immediately obvious. Little things, at first. She had an appointment with a doctor about a chest complaint and found that he was extra solicitous. When she returned for a check-up, and the complaint had been solved, he was ecstatic. Going up a flight of stairs, she dropped her bag, spilling her belongings all over the place. A man stooped to help her collect her things. Attracted by the commotion, another stopped and joined in. And then another, and another. Soon enough they were fighting over her phone, her compact, and her notebook – snatching them from each other's hands in their eagerness to return them to her.

People began seeking her out to tell her stories. They needed her to know that they would have done things differently, if only they had known. She found she never needed to say anything to these people. Once they had said their piece they would leave, seeming always to be satisfied.

At first, she took some enjoyment in this extra interest, but soon enough it became a burden. She couldn't go five minutes without someone opening their heart to her or crossing the street to open a door for her.

She decided that enough was enough and started provoking the people who disrupted her day. First, neglecting to thank people for their kindnesses, then, becoming bolder, making dismissive noises. In reply to people's confessions, she would shake her head and say, 'I don't know about that'. But nothing she did or said seemed to discourage anyone. Despite her rudeness, people continued to leave their encounters with her with a beatific look plastered across their faces.

Then one fine spring day, she was walking through the park to meet a friend when she was dazzled by the low afternoon sun, filtering through the branches of the trees. She raised her hand to her eyes and blinked. Blinked again. And she felt as though in that pause, between one moment and the next, the world had slipped. Something was out of joint, but it was impossible to pinpoint what. The smell of cut grass suddenly more intense and the colours ever so slightly brighter. She stopped and squinted, closing one eye after the other. Voids spiralled from the edge of her vision to the centre: persistent changeling fireflies that obscured the world when her eyes were open, and flared against the darkness when they were closed.

She stumbled on, looking for shade, and as she found a bench she was hit by a wave of nausea. All of the signals through which she normally received and interpreted the world were crowded by static, and the noise was making her feel sick.

The last thing she wanted, at this moment, was for someone to seek her out and gratify themselves by attending to whatever needs they projected onto her. She shut her eyes, clenched her fists, and waited for it to pass.

When it did, it was displaced by pain. Hot and searing, a pick-axe pressed against her temple. But at least now she could move without the danger of being sick. Clenching her teeth against the pain, she staggered home to her flat.

The next day she woke feeling drugged, like some sensory limit had been breached and her brain was running at reduced capacity. The migraine wasn't over and she was still sensitive to light, so when she did eventually manage to lever herself out of bed and go out to do some shopping, the first thing she did was buy a pair of sunglasses.

She took to wearing them everywhere, a safety blanket against another attack. And in the weeks afterwards, she noticed that people were paying her less attention. She could take the bus without hearing about someone's messy divorce, and, at the office, get on with her work without being interrupted by constant and unwanted offers of help.

One day, rushing to get to work, she forgot to put on her sunglasses as she was leaving the house. She was cursing herself as she sat down on the bus, fearful of another migraine, when a man seated in front of her turned and began to tell her about his relationship with his estranged daughter. *Here we go again*, she thought to herself. It was when he started talking about being left at a playground by his own mother when he was a child that she snapped.

'Enough! I don't want to hear about it!' She sat back in her seat, shocked but exhilarated by her alacrity. The man paused, and she watched, horrified, as that beatific smile, the one that until so recently had followed her wherever she went, unfolded across his face.

'Until I met you,' he said, 'I don't think anyone ever saw me as I truly am.'

'You are a shitty person,' she screamed, 'living a selfish life!'

His smile didn't shift. He rang the bell and got off at the next stop without another word.

At work, she was unable to concentrate. She kept replaying the encounter over and over, trying to track what she had said onto his response. It didn't make any sense. Who would react in such a way to obvious hostility? Was he a masochist? Simply deranged? But as she looked back, and compared this encounter to all of those that had gone before, it slowly dawned on her that he hadn't heard her at all. It wasn't that he saw what he was; rather he saw himself as he wished to be seen.

I let the silence hang between us, waiting for your response. It went on for so long that I began to wonder if you had been listening at all.

'Is that it?' you said, finally. You turned your head to me, smiling, wide-eyed and ironical.

'How would you have finished it?' I asked.

You laughed, shook your head and turned away, staring up at the ceiling. 'Is it supposed to have some kind of moral?'

'You tell me.'

'I was sure that she was going to fall in love.' You propped yourself up on one elbow and poked me in the ribs. 'You know, with someone who saw her for who *she* really is.'

'It's not a fairy tale.'

'No? Then what? A fable?' You rolled onto your back. 'You want to know how I see you? There are simpler ways of asking.'

'That's not what it's about.' I was offended that you could think I would be so obvious. Or that you had called me out on it.

'In any case, that's not how it feels.'

'What do you mean?'

'The way you described her migraine. That's not how mine feel at all.'

Sam and I stand in the ruins of Elsing Spital, catching our breath. We have scurried from the roundabout through Moorgate to the safer ground of the City; the warren of streets that huddle against the ghostly outline of the old walls. Across the roadway, there is a single planted bed, crocuses and snow-drops. I wonder whether the bulbs have survived because of some quirk of geography, protected by the edifices of blown glass that crowd it, or whether someone has returned, to breathe them back to life.

I give proper consideration, for the first time, to what Sam thinks of me. It's a habit I've lost again, since you left. I always felt like it was something that you loved holding over me, that I could never know exactly how a migraine felt.

It comes back to me that Sam used the word 'capable'.

Considering the state I was in, it's hard to fathom what he might have meant by it. He shuffles his feet, watching me. 'Where are you from?' he asks.

'Haggerston, all my life,' I say. 'What about you?'

'I grew up in Essex.'

'Have you been back?'

'It was on the route everyone was taking to the coast, the place where I grew up. I went once.'

'Why did you come back?'

He smiles but then narrows his eyes, staring at something over my shoulder. As I turn, following his gaze, he grabs my arm and says, 'Let's keep going. I'll tell you along the way.'

We sweep eastwards along that rampart cum roadway. I'm already thinking of how I might make my debut aurashow. I make a mental note – perhaps I could layer my fortification aura over a timelapse of the city skyline, a play on the buried Roman fort at the heart – and then Sam directs me down Love Lane.

'I'd been away too long,' he says. 'And by the time I had got there the place I knew had disappeared. It was the past I wanted to visit, not the place, I suppose.'

'Do you remember, when everyone thought that the implants might make it impossible for people to forget?' For the first time, there was the possibility that you could remember everything. Hit capture and start the creation of a lossless record which – with the help of image-recognition AI – could be endlessly recalled and analysed by any criteria you might imagine. Provided it was recorded, every interaction with a particular person could be replayed simply by bringing to mind the person's face and allowing an algorithm to summon it from the data.

It is thinking of this story I made up for you that brings it to mind. Our memories are the story we tell to ourselves, of ourselves; the function which, through accumulation, the self emerges. Central to this emergence is the ability to forget.

'I still worry about that,' Sam says. 'How often do you have that thing switched on, anyway? Are you recording right now?'

People feared that, without any ability to forget, there would be a mass identity crisis. Being forced to confront all our blunders and petty cruelties, our emotional missteps and miscommunications, would shred the tissue of half-truths and screen memories which formed the patchwork of an 'authentic' self, which allowed us to face the world.

'Why would anyone want to remember everything?' I say.

Sam laughs – looks at me slantwise, studying my face carefully. 'I can't think of anything to say to that, other than: what is it that you're trying to forget?'

We come out on Cheapside, a sudden throng. The arpeggio peal of Bow bells rings out, every note an icepick against my temple.

'You'd have thought they would give that a rest,' I say. 'The day after a storm.'

'On their busiest day?' He pauses for a moment, in the flow of people. 'When the wind blows the right direction, you can hear them in Haggerston now,' Sam says.

'I've never noticed.'

The gathering of people in St Paul's churchyard, which began with the headaches, has by now spilled out onto the roads that radiate from the cathedral. Pilgrims are setting up trestle tables and unpacking trinkets.

There are imports from all the way along the estuary, mostly dragged by hand. Tubs full of oysters brought up from the beds out at Mersea; car batteries and generators pulled from hospitals and office blocks; clothes scavenged from empty houses in the ghost towns that ring the city and line the river as it winds towards the channel. There are bushels of dried feverfew, mugwort, peppermint and willow, any herb that holds even the remotest claim to relieve the symptoms of migraine. It has become a stopping point even for those who aren't interested in the cathedral; an opportunity for those who, like me, trade labour for food to cash in their surplus.

Alongside these herbalists: acupuncturists and chiropractors line up behind their chairs.

Sam pulls me in the opposite direction of the cathedral, towards the pealing bells.

As he does, I catch a glimpse of a face in the crowd. One of the men who had been talking to the crowd outside Suleymaniye mosque in Hoxton. In the instant that I make the connection between these two sightings, a third image presents itself: the same face glimpsed out of the corner of my eye on Old Street. It's only now, the third time I have seen him today, that I realise who he is.

But it couldn't be – the person whose face looms out of my memory; he left. Would he still even recognise me? I tug at my chin, my five-day stubble; run my hand over my cropped hair. By the time I look again, the crowd has closed around him and he has disappeared.

In the churchyard itself, more tables are laid out, stacked high with loose papers. Crusty-looking men in fingerless gloves flick methodically through the yellowing and mildewed mountains.

'My people!' Sam says, gesturing wide with his arms. One man looks up for a moment, snarling at the interruption, and then returns to his excavation. 'They have it all here. Maps, plans, ordinances, inventories, planning applications, archaeological surveys – every foundation and plague pit, lift shaft and sealed-up sewer.'

'What are you here looking for, anyway?' I scan the crowd, but he has disappeared once more.

'An old friend.' He starts to move between the tables. 'You do have to be a little bit careful of this lot. They can be quite capricious. One bookseller I used to buy from on the Waste – this was long before the weather – had carts that he hung with canvas. He'd been in the forces, I think, had that ramrod bearing. We'd all line up and at a certain point he'd throw back the covers. It was every man for himself. We'd be fighting one another for manuscripts and broadsides, playing tug-of-war with eighteenth-century volumes with weak hinges. But if he caught you at it, he would take the item from your hands and tear it up in front of your eyes. It didn't matter whether it was a shopping list or a Doré plate, he'd tear it to shreds just to teach you a lesson.'

As Sam is talking, I continue to examine the faces in the crowd. Perhaps I imagined it. I can't separate the tickly feeling I have that we were being followed, from the general unease I feel because of his manic eccentricity.

'Wait here, just two minutes.' He rushes off. I begin to leaf through a pile of mildewed papers on the table in front of me. It is a poster stall. Pin-ups of forgotten celebrities and glamour models mixed in with art deco and nouveau reproductions, line drawings and Matisse knock-offs – the collective detritus of every millennial and Gen-X flatshare from before the weather. I watch Sam as he pulls the plastic package from his coat and thrusts the papers at the bookseller, a severe man in his middle age sporting a shabby waistcoat and a rather threadbare moustache.

An intrusion: something in the angle of his arm as he holds the paper to the light, made that old image present itself – a body falling to the earth. I look up to the sky and the image persists: his profiled face against the high, hazy cloud. I press my fingers into my eyes until it slowly fades.

When I look back, the bookseller is shaking his head; Sam is getting more and more animated, trying to persuade him of something. The man is holding out the papers, trying to get Sam to take them back. Eventually, he simply lets go of the package and holds up his hands, watching as they drift to the floor in the space between them.

'Seen anything you like the look of?' The poster stall owner steps in front of me. I realise I am still absent-mindedly flicking through the posters on the table.

When I look back Sam is tearing at his hair in disbelief. He snatches the papers up and waves them in front of the severe man, who has raised one hand in something like apology and turned away.

'You going to trade anything, or what?'

It occurs to me I could just go. Slip away and make my way to you alone. What exactly am I waiting for?

But this sighting, of a person who I thought I was free of, makes me hesitate. It makes me fearful of continuing alone. The distractions of Sam's obscure purpose are giving me time to think.

Before I can think any more on it, Sam appears at my elbow.

'Idiots,' he mutters, scowling at the poster seller. 'Short-sighted, pigeon-chested, bed-wetting idiots! My whole life I've been thwarted by them.' He throws up his hands, then pats the pocket on his chest. 'Come on, we're almost there.'

A storm brought us together, so it's only fitting that another was the trigger for our first fight.

At that point I felt like my attempts to find a common cause between Malik, you and me – to bring the two parallel worlds into focus – were going well. Even if I was holding you at arm's length from one another. I went to see him because he said he had a new product for you to try.

I found him in his garage by the station, in the back, tinkering with a shortwave radio. Aid agencies still used them. Scavengers too. Malik liked to listen in on both.

'Managed to get some tea-tree oil,' he said. 'Dead stock from a Boots depot that somehow survived till now. Reckon it gives a little extra spice.'

Since the Freeze, the huge fulfilment warehouses ringing the

M25 had already undergone a transformation as radical as the Valley of the Kings. I wondered, idly, what tourists three thousand years from now would make of those huge, vaulted monuments.

He passed the stick to me. He'd smartened up the packaging. Vinyl stickers he had fabricated somehow.

I picked up an old-fashioned barometer. It was like the face of an antique clock, but where the numbers should have been were copperplate letters, ranging from 'STORMY' at seven o'clock, to 'VERY DRY' at five o'clock. At twelve o'clock the word *Change* was set in italics, ornamented with extravagant serifs.

'Did you ever get much interest in these?' I asked.

'No, it's strange.'

'Maybe I should get one for Luna,' I said, holding a particularly ornate one up to the light. 'But, then, I suppose it makes sense that you wouldn't want to know if one was coming for you. If you couldn't do anything about it.' I put it back down among the clutter.

After a few moments silence, Malik said: 'Have to say, I'm surprised she's interested in you.'

'What do you mean?' I said, snorting.

'Guys like you and me, you know. It's tough out here.'

'Tough out here?' I repeated. It didn't sound like something Malik would say. More like something he had heard. I rolled my eyes, and absent-mindedly picked up a brass candlestick. 'What are you on about?'

'Just saying, I think it's cool. That Luna sees through all the negativity that's out there about us. Doesn't look down on you, just because you're different.'

I groaned. 'Malik. Fuck's sake, mate. You need to find a new hobby.' I let the candlestick clatter to the floor.

Malik had started following some guys on the feeds who had positioned themselves in opposition to the flood of migraine-related content – the self-styled 'ableists'.

Most of these guys were back-to-the-land types: scuffed Barbour coats, Bible quotes and side partings. Extolling the virtues of hard work and restoring your circadian rhythms. It was old media stuff, easy to see through. Gobber was different. Before the Freeze, there was a low-key sensation when the phrase 'Nat has herpes' started appearing in massive letters on disused buildings, train sidings, and other hard-to-reach places all around the city.

It had been a kind of urban myth; the general assumption was that most of the tags had been sprayed by copy-cats, a self-replicating joke. But after the Thaw, Gobber outed himself as the mastermind. I was unconvinced, but no one contested it. It went from being a tag to a brand. He started streaming his urban art projects, spraying using programmed drones. He went viral after tagging the dome of St Paul's. His cackling laugh – as vicars and stewards circled below, trying to smash his drones out of the sky with brooms – became his signature, endlessly looped over the clips of other tricksters.

He was evasive. He refused to ever explain what the tag meant, who Nat was. So, it had been adopted by ableists on the feeds and became a kind of digital handshake.

We'd both known him, before, during the Freeze, but under another name, Gino. I hadn't made the connection until Malik had shared some of the clips with me, a few months before. Ever since, he'd begun to drop some wild theories into conversation.

'You been watching this Gobber shit again? Is that where all this men's rights stuff is coming from?'

'Does Luna ever mention him?'

'Why would she?'

'Just wondering, I guess ... what she thinks of him. When am I going to meet her, by the way?'

Whatever he was driving at, I didn't want to hear it. 'What's this?' I said, picking up a freezer bag full of beige powder.

'Pea protein,' he said. 'I can get you some if you like.'

'You're all right, mate. I'll leave the peas to the pod people.'

He laughed and went back to applying stickers to his PrikStiks.

He had started purifying his own water, convinced that the supplies at the local co-op were spiked with oestrogen. Always a big guy, he worked out a lot more seriously, rigging up a whole series of bars and weights in his garage.

It only took two swipes to go from watching a prankster spraying a cathedral to finding yourself listening to a guy in a vest top talking about how the migraine attacks were part of a wider attempt to feminise culture. To defang alpha go-getters, stop them from taking what was rightly theirs.

Gino was a person from a time that I wanted to forget. But in his new guise, despite myself, I could understand the appeal. It could feel oppressive, to have to live on someone else's time. And the Gobber schtick was funny. It was childish but he *was* funny. With him, at least, it was knowing. Which meant you knew where you stood. After all that had happened, I found some of the sensitivity around this new sickness a little absurd. Still, with Malik I felt the need to play this down. I felt that he was using Gobber to prick me about you, but at that point I didn't understand it.

'Have you been seeing anyone?' I asked.

'Not really. Not since Elodie.'

'Over in Hoxton? What happened with that?'

'She said I was hostile. That I didn't listen.'

'Wasn't into your whole Hulk Hogan flex, then?' I said, reaching out to pump his bicep.

He batted me away. 'You might have had more luck with her.'

'Yeh?'

'You could have run her errands, picked up after her.'

'Like I do with Luna, you mean?' I went over, trying to catch his eye.

He just shrugged, carried on stickering, stacking up the sticks.

'You saying I'm some kind of lapdog? Is that it?'

'Just looking out for you, man. Would hate to see a friend of mine taken advantage of.'

'Just because I don't buy into your school-shooter shit doesn't mean I'm getting walked all over.' I shook the box he was filling, rattling the sticks inside. 'She's been pretty good to you, too. Featuring this stuff on the feeds.'

'And whose idea was that, then? It's not like she hasn't benefitted, too.' He paused, continued more gently. 'Just don't let her forget that.' He shut the box and handed it to me. 'That's all I'm saying.'

I was in a pretty foul mood when I got back to the flat, the taste of that conversation still in my mouth. You had been brittle the past couple of days, snapping at me, and making me feel generally underfoot. We were still getting used to one another, in the negotiation phase of co-habitation.

We hadn't even really had a conversation, as such, about me moving in. I'd simply stopped going home. We kept making plans, every day, to get together in the evening. Then, one day you went out before I woke, and left me a key on the bedside table. That was that: we stopped making plans and getting together became the default. You had been to my place but yours was bigger. Besides that, your place was where you made your work, so by defaulting to staying at your place I thought I was respecting that. In this case, I think the ease between us was increased by the fact that we didn't discuss it; the seamlessness of it simply coming to be burnished the sense that we were meant for one another. But I suppose it did establish a pattern of communication, one that perhaps doomed us.

When I opened the door, I could hear you crashing around in the kitchen. I went through to find you pulling mugs off their hooks and putting them back up, one by one, in size order. I watched, waiting for you to finish, to acknowledge my presence.

You turned, not meeting my eyes, and took a dishcloth in your hands, folding and refolding. 'I told you. The mugs. They need to go in size order.'

'OK,' I said, pausing to put down my keys and the things I had collected from Malik, and from the co-op, on the table. 'I'm sorry, I guess. Must have forgotten.'

You didn't say anything, but put the dishcloth on the table and began to retie your hair, drawing it severely against her scalp.

'Look,' I said, gesturing at the food on the table. 'Managed to get us some aubergines and Malik has got these new PrikStiks, they've got tea tree in them which he reckons . . .'

'It's just not much to ask,' you said. 'Is it? For the mugs to be put back on the hooks in size order.'

'I said that I'm sorry, I don't know what . . .'

'It's a small thing,' you interrupted again. 'It's not like I'm particular about everything. I'm trying not to make a big deal out of it but . . .'

I snapped. 'How about you go and get your own fucking food? Eh? Instead of moping around the place all day waiting for me to bring it.'

'If I'm such a *burden*,' you said, waving your hands in the air, 'why spend all your time here? Haunting my flat with your holey socks and your . . .'

I swept the aubergine off the table against the wall. Seeing no other option, I stormed from the room, slamming the front door behind me. I had forgotten how to manage conflict in any way other than to immediately escalate it. I was maladapted and unsure of myself. I knew I had to leave, to get out.

I walked quickly up Kingsland Road back towards Dalston. After a couple of minutes, I realised I had left my keys on the table and would have no way of getting back into my own place, but I didn't slow my pace. I needed to be on the move.

I stopped, turning in the road, unable to make a decision, and was rocked by a gust. Across the street from me, I heard the electronic whirr of storm shutters extending into place. In the distance, over the city, lightning was forking inside roiling clouds that seemed to have gathered out of nowhere. I was pulled and buffeted again, the hood of my coat lashing the side of my face. Either I had missed the early signs – the familiar electricity making my hair stand on end, the slight but sudden drop in temperature – or this one was coming in really fast.

I really didn't want to spend a night sleeping on compost bags. I took a deep breath and turned back into the wind, towards your apartment.

All the lights in the occupied flats and houses were being extinguished as I jogged back down the road, leaning into the wind. You could spot those blessed few who, like me, hadn't acquired a sudden sensitivity.

The wind was shooting along the crescent of Georgian townhouses opposite your block. Their shape created a turning column of air at the crossroads where they terminated, sucking up anything that flew into its path, and sending it spiralling into the air. Over time, we had all learned to instinctively avoid these danger points created by the idiosyncrasies of our local topographies and had become adept readers of the signs that marked them out: the deeper fissures in cracked tarmac, objects deposited on rooftops, evidence of the wind's passage like glacial erratics. As I watched, an abandoned shopping trolley was being slowly pulled towards its centre.

Power to the main door had already been shut off so I found the hidden fire key and got it open. Pulling it closed, the sudden drop in decibels was shocking.

The door to your apartment was unlocked. I let myself in and your bloodless face appeared around the corner, poking out from the kitchen into the corridor. The new PrikStik I had brought was in your hand.

'I'm sorry I . . .' I started.

'It hurts,' you interrupted, mashing the stick into your right temple before disappearing back into the kitchen.

'I know,' I said, following you. In the kitchen, the aubergine was half chopped and oil was fizzing and spitting in a pan on the hotplate. I switched it off and hauled you out of the chair you'd slumped into – inhaling the sour scent of your skin – leading you into the living room, your clammy hand in mine.

In the gloom I pulled all of the sofa cushions onto the floor and lay down next to you.

You leaned over and turned on the projector. 'Look,' you whispered in my ear. Eyes squeezed shut, you began to cast onto the ceiling as your implant captured, in real-time, what was unfolding behind your eyelids.

The backdrop was black with an almost imperceptible rose stain from the ambient light of the room, which lightened and darkened as you squeezed your eyes against the pain. A jagged inflorescence cut across the right-hand side; a drifting staircase of light. On either side a host of teardrops hovered, swelling and contracting, outlined by a shifting wash of red and green.

I smiled. 'Nature's rotten tricks.'

'The mugs,' you said. 'I'm sorry.'

'Don't worry, go to sleep.'

'It was coming, I could feel it.' You groaned. 'But you don't want to . . . You never want to . . .' You trailed off.

'I know.'

As I lay next to you I wondered: would it always be this way? If you picked a fight about the toilet seat or crumbs in the bed would I be tensed all day waiting for the storm to hit? Maybe it was me who needed a barometer, so I could separate the changing weather of our relationship from the whims of the changing air pressure. Easier though, not to know. To have the option to defer responsibility for the gathering clouds of your anger until the heavens opened. Or didn't.

Your breathing had slowed and steadied. Asleep already. I watched your chest rise and fall. Above, the aura was beginning to fade. The staircase had drifted upwards, touching the edge of the field. The light of it, once mercury bright, now shimmered pearlescent. The teardrops were contracting, the surface tension breaking as they collapsed in on themselves.

I wanted to meet this impulse of yours, to share something private, un-reconstructed, projected in real time, with something of my own. Something that described my own passage through the weather.

I knew just the thing. I hit play and skipped forward through the end of a news report. A sonorous Welsh voice came on, reciting a grave incantation.

WARNINGS OF GALES IN CROMARTY, FORTH, DOGGER, BISCAY.

You stirred and made a soft, animal sound.

AREA FORECAST FOR MIDNIGHT: VIKING, NORTH UTSIRE, SOUTH UTSIRE, FORTIES, FOUR TO SIX, RAIN, MODERATE OR GOOD, SHOWERS LATER . . .

I tuned out and closed my eyes, the gnomic and rhythmic words washing over us.

ROCKALL, MALIN, HEBRIDES, VARIABLE THREE AT FIRST IN MALIN, OTHERWISE SOUTHWEST FOUR TO SIX BECOMING CYCLONIC, GALE EIGHT TO STORM TEN LATER . . .

'Becoming cyclonic, a life, by Luna.' You murmured. I chuckled, stroking your hair. When the broadcast came to an end you poked me in the leg.

'More.'

'OK.'

NOW THE SHIPPING FORECAST ISSUED BY THE MET OFFICE ON BEHALF OF THE MARITIME AND COASTGUARD AGENCY. IT'S O-FIVE O-FIVE ON THURSDAY THE SIXTEENTH OF FEBRUARY . . .

*

The morning after, I woke early. In the kitchen, on the counter, I found a page torn from your notebook.

Migraine is . . . fractious, fussy, particular, snappish . . .
  ultimately apologetic
  Migraine is not . . . preventable, predictable, reasonable, accountable . . .
  ultimately permanent

I went back into the bedroom to where you lay on your side. I watched the steady rise and fall of your blanketed form, silhouetted in the light escaping from the edges of the curtains. I tried to imagine you, half-blind in the dark, scribbling in your notebook.

I laced up my trainers and, before the spell broke, let myself out into the silent street to run loops to reassure myself with the strength of my body.

*

The conversation with Malik in his garage had set a clock running, I just didn't realise it yet.

It was a long-running tradition that once a year, in the All Saints church in Haggerston, the clowns of London would gather to honour the memory of Joseph Grimaldi, and to mark the passing of members of their tribe who had died in the last twelve months.

I had been vaguely aware of this tradition – one of those pieces of local folklore that did the rounds at the pub – but I had no idea that it had survived the Freeze. Malik sent me a clip from Gobber's feed showing a virtual Jesus on the cross with his face powdered white and adorned with a red nose. 'Nat has herpes' was tattooed in spidery lettering on the inside of his outstretched bicep. As his signature cackle played, the words TRICKSTER TAKEOVER spiralled in from the top of the frame. He suggested that we come along.

I found an old video from before the Freeze, showing one of the services. It started with an interview in front of the church: a man in full make-up – a multi-coloured skullcap with a propeller pinned into his receding grey hair – solemnly reassuring the off-camera interviewer that it was going to be a 'light-hearted occasion' and 'full of fun'.

In the church, clowns filled the first five rows of pews, decked in every interpretation of the spirit of Grimaldi imaginable: harlequin jackets, purple wigs, huge floral bloomers. Readings and hymns alternated with performances – juggling, puppets and mime. A man dressed as a jester policeman gave a eulogy to one of his fallen comrades, banging his squeaky truncheon on the lectern to punctuate his tribute to a man who was a 'credit to the calling'.

We were never a church-going family, but I'd always go along with Mum to Midnight Mass on Christmas Eve, around the corner at St Peter's – the huge church in de Beauvoir. She loved carols, and she loved pointing out all the old men who had come straight from last orders, nodding off in the pews. The combination of Anglican forced cheeriness with the exaggerated melancholy of the clowning that was on view in the video somehow recalled the spirit of those Christmas visits with her, so I think in some ways it felt like an opportunity to be with you and her together.

There was also a part of me that wanted to see Gino's

transformation for myself. His presence on the feeds was so totally at odds with the person I had known during the Freeze that it was hard to reconcile.

Also, you and Malik had to meet eventually. The thought made me nervous: I was still reluctant to relinquish the illusion of control I had over the self-image that I presented to you. But by holding out for much longer, I ran the risk of making you both feel I was embarrassed of you, rather than of myself.

I showed you the video I'd watched and asked you whether you were interested in coming along.

'A church full of clowns . . .' you said, with a smile. 'What's the worst that could happen?' Since the argument we had both been careful around each other, eager to please.

I had never paid much attention to this other church, set slightly back from Haggerston Road. Most of the boards that had been put in to protect the leaded windows were still in place, and the gaps in the slate roof were patched with sheets of black plastic.

'We could just go for a walk with Malik,' you said.

'Second thoughts?' I was having them too.

'It's not often we get a day like this.'

The brilliant sunshine and mild air did make the prospect of sitting for an hour in a gloomy, run-down church feel extremely unappealing. It recalled those endless early summer days before the Freeze.

A small group in traditional clown gear huddled to one side of the door.

'Come on,' I said, taking your hand. 'Let's find Malik.'

I spotted him, just outside the gate, talking with some people

I didn't know. They were all wearing some kind of flower on their chest.

I caught his eye and he waved. We went over and you introduced yourself.

'What's that on your chest?' I asked.

'Have a look,' he said. I leaned in and he pulled down on the flower's stem, sending a jet of water shooting into my eye.

You snorted with laughter and I staggered backwards, spluttering, as the tinny sound of Gobber's cackling laugh filled the air.

'These guys were giving them out,' Malik said, gesturing to the people he had been talking to, a few of whom I vaguely recognised from the neighbourhood. 'Fucking hilarious.'

Inside, it took some moments for my eyes to adjust to the low light, cast by the single unboarded window. In place of pews were rows of plastic garden chairs. Someone was playing the Benny Hill theme tune on the organ.

We took seats near the back. The room was divided in two. The right-hand side taken up by the ragged band of clowns, in their cobbled together costumes. On the left was a group of men, in their twenties and thirties, unremarkable aside from the vinyl flowers pinned to their chests.

'Apparently Gobber is giving a sermon,' Malik said.

'A sermon?' I said. 'Why?'

He shrugged and gave me a knowing smile.

Before I could say anything else, voices rose in front of us. Heads began to turn to the back of the church.

'Did Malik say he's giving a sermon?'

I widened my eyes at you and mouthed, 'Sorry!' You smiled and shook your head, looking a little nervous.

The procession filed in. The vicar, in tattered robes, a purple bowler hat balanced jauntily on his head his sole concession to the occasion. Behind him came a bulky, slouching man, dressed in a hoody and jeans. Malik elbowed me in the ribs: 'There he is'.

Gobber fist-bumped a few of his acolytes and took a seat in the front row.

As the vicar called us all to our feet and began the liturgy, I studied the back of Gobber's head. I could scarcely credit that it was Gino. Everything – his whole embodiment – had changed. The man I knew was rangy – viper-like in his movements. This creatine-toned gym bro in front of me was almost unrecognisable. But underneath it all, there was still the same self-assurance, the same ominous sanguinity.

After the preamble and a couple of prayers, a clown was invited to the altar, where he climbed onto a unicycle and gave a desultory juggling performance.

Next came a hymn, which the clowns accompanied with great honking and hawing of their novelty trumpets and kazoos, I began to relax.

But just then, as we took our seats, Gobber – his transformation was so total that he seemed even to have shed his old name – made his way slowly to the altar. He paused to survey the room before lowering his hood.

'The Lord God took man and put him in the garden of Eden to work it and keep it.' He closed the Bible on the lectern in front of him. I was as confused as I was nervous: the man I knew hadn't exactly been a gospel scholar.

'You were right,' you whispered. 'Hilarious.'

Malik shushed.

'Before the fall, there was work. Even in paradise: work. From where, then, have we suddenly developed this notion that work is born of sin? That to be able-bodied, to expend your energy in pursuit of your own betterment, is somehow shameful?'

He took in the church with his outstretched arms.

'Instead we valorise sickness. We valorise idleness. We spend our days glued to the feeds, celebrating those that repackage their malaise for us to digest. Over and over.' He struck the lectern with his fist, punctuating each word into the charged silence that had fallen over the church. 'While those who rise above the general affliction, we who remain bodily resolute, are punished for it. For what? For trying to bring back the world we have lost?' He was sweating now. 'We work for what? For our own profit?' This time, into the stunned hush, one side of the aisle shouted in response: 'No!' Gobber smiled, greasily satisfied. 'No, we work to support those who refuse to support themselves.'

I could sense your presence next to me by your stillness. A silence I didn't want to turn towards. While part of me was disgusted, there was also a small part that was perversely thrilled.

One of the clowns, a woman seated in the front row, stood and walked down the aisle towards the back of the church. All the young guys wearing the flower pennants were turning to one another, their faces contorted into the tongue out, crosseyed expression that Malik had turned on me. They began to hoot. The woman turned and, just before she slipped out the door, shouted 'shameful!' above the din.

The atmosphere felt finely poised. On the face of it, the woman's reaction might have seemed a little extreme. On the face of it, what he was saying was disrespectful, but not particularly shocking. But each era has its taboos, and speaking out against the sick is the defining one in ours.

There was something so insidious about the set-up. What characterised the clowns' charm, what had drawn me to the church, was the solemnity behind the absurdity – using humour to draw out something sincere. It was oddly touching. Gobber was doing the opposite, using irony as a Trojan horse, a foil for deniability.

Gobber held out his hands for calm. I was strangely transfixed, so much so that I wasn't at this point considering how this was landing with you. I wonder now, had you heard this little speech before?

'If I speak,' he said, throwing his hands up by his ears in mock surrender, 'of the real sacrifice we make, then I'm in trouble. If I speak of the sacrifice that able-bodied men everywhere are making, to live in a world defined by sickness and weakness – men who, after five years of vicious winter, are punished for their survival, for their strength – if I speak of this, then . . .'

He paused. He had said more in the past few minutes than he had for weeks at a time, when I had known him during the Freeze, when his reticence was a part of his menace.

More and more of the clowns were standing up to leave. One threw a juggling ball which struck the vicar, who fled across the transept, crashing into empty chairs in the choir stalls. Some of the young men were crossing the aisle, fists raised, that absurd expression frozen on their faces.

Once again Gobber threw up his hands and shouted, 'People! Friends . . .' There was a break in the swelling tension as heads swung back in his direction. 'What will our honoured guest think?'

He lowered his hands, 'That's right, we are lucky enough to have among us one of these merchants of idleness.' Tilting his head, he adopted the cross-eyed emoji rictus. 'A famous migraineur!' A jeer rose up in the crowd, cut through with more cries of 'shame!' from the clowns. 'Luna, it's so good to see you. Why don't you stand, and make yourself known?'

People in the rows in front of us were turning their heads, scanning the faces of their neighbours. At the sound of your name the trance that I had fallen into, brought on by the jarring strangeness of Gino's transformation, broke. I turned to you, and all the blood had drained from your face.

I could feel the crowd's awareness gathering around us like heat.

I looked back and forth between you and Gobber where he stood, still, at the lectern, his arms wide. His eyes had found yours. A moment later, they found mine.

I took your hand, and without another word, we pushed past Malik and fled from the church.

The look of terror on your face . . . I should have known. I was so focused on my past with Gino, on concealing it from you, that I was blind to your own. Part of me wanted you to know, otherwise surely I wouldn't have asked you to the church, part of you must have wanted me to know, otherwise you wouldn't have come.

We ran all the way to Kingsland Road. We were howling – really whooping – that laugh that only rises when your lungs are burning. The laugh that doesn't say 'how funny!' but instead 'how close!'

As Sam and I cross the churchyard from the stalls towards the cathedral steps, I think of the flight from that other church. The words SOLIDARITY NOT CHARITY are sprayed in huge and uneven letters across the ground.

Sam pulls up, pointing them out.

'Pious bastards. Everywhere.'

I laugh. 'What were you expecting?'

'Not this kind of piety. A different brand. I thought, at least here, we might get a break from this sententious crap.'

'Sententious. Wow. I'm impressed.'

'Oh, do shut up.'

'Are you some kind of . . . I don't know . . . man of letters?'

The tenor of our conversation feels strangely at odds with my growing sense of dread. But the place is heaving. Looking over my shoulder, I can't see either of the two men who I am, by now, certain are following us. I can't imagine that they'll confront us in such a public space and I am hopeful that they won't imagine that we're here for the service. I take Sam by the elbow and lead him on. I'm starting to feel a degree of comfort from his company. Not because I believe that he'll protect me, more that he is so absurd and unserious that it's hard to believe that anything could go seriously wrong while I'm with him.

The pilgrims gathered here are more homogenous, tending towards the pious, than the ones who were gathered in the roads leading towards the cathedral. In the porchway, two men dressed in hooded robes, decorated with a constellation of stars from shoulder to wrist, are handing a pamphlet to people as they file into the church.

'What's wrong with it?' I say, gesturing back at the graffiti. 'Seems like quite an easy sentiment to get behind, if you ask me.'

'Disingenuous claptrap. Dreamed up by a bunch of hypo-crites, who want to forget how they spent the last five years. Where was the solidarity when we were freezing to death?' He shrugs me off – I hadn't realised quite how firmly I was holding his elbow – and turns to give me a look loaded with expectation.

'Is that why I've never seen you in Dalston Square, then?'

'You've seen me,' Sam says, still eying me carefully. 'Maybe not in Dalston Square, but you've seen me. It will come to you.'

As one of the men turns to pick up a new pile of pamphlets, I catch a glimpse of the back of his robe, emblazoned with a circle of golden stitching, in the middle of which is a figure of a woman stitched in blue, with her palms held outwards.

This is one of the images I've seen stencilled onto the walls all through the city and along Cheapside, competing with the

101

copycat clown flowers sprayed by Gobber's followers, and the slogan sprayed on the paving in front of us. One of the stalls at the approach to Bow Bells had been selling magnets and pin badges, with LEDs lighting the circular backdrop – a tacky halo.

I've been hoping that what I'll see inside will be some kind of antidote, some kind of counter spell, to the scene we saw together at the church in Haggerston.

I cast around, trying to catch sight of the face that is now haunting me, in the swell of pilgrims. The crowd is thick. I take a deep breath. Forget it. Press on.

Sam is pushing and shoving his way through the people, glancing over his shoulder.

'Come on, Ellis, I thought you wanted to see this.'

He grabs my jacket and pulls me to the front of the queue to enter the church. I automatically take the piece of paper held out to me by one of the robed figures. The word 'Scivias' is printed on the front cover in elaborate text above a greyscale rendering of the image embroidered on the robes. At the bottom: the name 'Hildegard of Bingen'.

That slogan sprayed on the paving stones outside of St Paul's, and Sam's reaction to it, captures something of the legacy of the Freeze. The sense of shame that is embedded in this new solidarity that it proclaims.

After the pandemonium of the initial months, at the onset of the snow my life settled into an altogether more civilised pattern. I still believe that it is in almost everyone's nature to want to live in harmony with those around them. To want to find a way of living from each according to their ability, to each according to their needs.

The killing by London Fields was an accident. Malik and I talked it over endlessly, even if I wasn't able to confide in anyone else. And part of me was able to accept this. I don't say this to dismiss it, but I'm starting to realise that it's not the act itself but the grain of fear that it planted in me, and the permissiveness that stemmed from that fear, that I've come to be most ashamed of.

The nearest aid distribution centre to me was the one in Haggerston station. It made sense to locate it there, at least while they could still keep the elevated tracks clear. I threw myself into helping out. Going from spending my days trawling abandoned houses for trinkets to sorting aid parcels felt like a step towards atonement.

The food arrived and we worked together to process and divide it up, each taking a role according to their abilities, and with the supplies offered to each according to their needs.

Organisation has never been my strong suit, so I didn't put myself forward for any of the administrative roles. But I was strong and willing. I was happy to unload sacks of potatoes and bags of pasta, to roll and stack the cylinders of Calor Gas.

Scarcity is what everyone fears, at the moment of disaster, but the fact was that – because of the exodus of people – there was more than enough to go around for the people who had decided to stay.

This is the spirit that now animates the farms, the co-ops.

But while a majority of people are inclined to live in harmony with those around them, it only takes a very small active minority to activate the avaricious side in all of us that is borne out of the fear of avariciousness in others – create scarcity where there is none and then exploit it in others.

This was where Gino came in. I always wondered why I'd never seen you there, but now it all makes more sense.

I'll come back to him. There was another arrival, just before he insinuated himself into our lives, who I realise now was in some ways just as important.

Limpet was some kind of nervous sighthound. She simply appeared, one day, at the station. I suppose she had been left behind by her owner in the exodus and had the sense to seek out warmth with other humans. She stuck around and was adopted by the rotating volunteers who ran the centre.

Whenever I arrived, she would make straight for me, following me around the whole time I remained: unpacking and stacking tins, measuring out dried pasta from large sacks into smaller ones. Because of her attentiveness, and because of a slight quirk in her gait that would only make itself known when she broke into a run, someone nicknamed her Limpet. It stuck.

The real reason that she was fixated on me, why she would notice my arrival before anyone else, was an infection on my shins. The attention that was interpreted by everyone else as affection was really just animal curiosity. Limpet would bound over to me to bury her nose into the fabric of my snowsuit, performing a series of short and sharp inhalations, wagging her abbreviated tail so hard that her whole rump swayed with it.

It made me feel exposed, vaguely embarrassed, to be thrust into this awareness of the meat of my body, its teeming vitality, made otherwise invisible by the folds of cotton and nylon. I didn't know how to deal with this exposure, Limpet's insistence that I confront my flesh. I hid her interest by showering her with attention: pats and rubs which began to associate, in her mind, her curiosity with the affection that everyone else had mistaken it for, generating a genuine bond.

I'd developed the folliculitis a few months after it began to snow. I have always suffered from sensitive skin, streaks of inflammation that perform a slow-motion semaphore, a gnomic transcription of what was happening below the surface. As you know by now, if I'm coming down with a cold, the skin around my eyes and mouth begins to itch. If I ever stay out too late, for too many nights, or let myself get too stressed with work, the backs of my knees and insides of my elbows flare, the blood filling the well-worn highways of histamine response.

In this case, it was the snowsuit. Always too hot or too cold, my body always slightly sheened with sweat from the exertion – a self-generated humidity that it was impossible to prevent or escape.

The weather made it worse. The unrelenting wind hurling itself across the top of the screed of snow, drying and chapping any skin left exposed. And then there was uncertainty. The sense of the days slipping by without purpose or purchase.

I noticed it on my left shin first: a spray of reddened hair follicles. It didn't hurt, exactly, but it was hot in a way that made me want to lay my palm over the top of it, to curl my fingers around my calf and form a seal, as if I could draw the heat away. A couple of days later the follicles bloomed white with tiny pinheads and the red inflammation deepened, to a vivid purple.

I tried lavender, thyme, tea-tree oil – all of those remedies that arose from a supposed a connection to the land which we had been slowly unbraiding. In the years before the snow started, the city was declared the largest urban forest on earth. A tree for every inhabitant, almost. As if that were even almost enough. The Freeze was a quick lesson in the cruelty of optimism.

None of these remedies worked because I wasn't able to do anything about the root causes. Ambient stress, poor diet, badly heated and insulated housing – the same old factors elevated to new extremes. Nevertheless, most of the time, I was able to forget these blooms on my shins. Wrapped and shrouded, my body had an anonymous quality, falling below the notice of others and thereby my own.

All apart from Limpet. I always wondered what richness she experienced there, at the interface of my skin. How did she experience it? Where did one end and the other begin? I began to welcome this secret, held between us, of my body's otherness. Of its existence as something of which I was simply a contingent part.

And then one day, quite soon after Gino's arrival, Limpet disappeared. She had become such a fixture that I simply assumed that she would reappear. But as the days turned into weeks it became clear that she wasn't coming back.

With the loss of Limpet, I lost her easy nose for the fact of our porousness, her simple delight in something that for us was so hard learned.

It wasn't until I met you that – in the blush of that first touch, when my blood rushed to meet yours, straining at the skin – for the first time since Limpet showed me the intimacy of infection, I remembered my body.

*

By the time Gino arrived, I suppose we were looking for someone to follow. His skill was in providing the most fertile ground for any grain of fear to flourish. He drifted in, just as I had, and was accepted in the same spirit of togetherness.

He was quiet and unassuming, which is utterly at odds with the persona he has developed since the Thaw. At first he worked hard, but with a watchfulness that made me uneasy.

The corruption started small, keeping a few things back from the aid shipments at his encouragement. Malik saw more quickly than me what it was all leading to, raising his eyebrows as I stowed an extra pair of snowshoes, an extra bag of rice. But it seemed harmless. A series of small, discrete acts, rather than the first steps down a new path.

This was different from what Malik and I had been doing when the snow first started to fall; it was one thing to strip useless consumer goods from shops abandoned by the multinationals who had been profiting from a distance, another to steal food from our neighbours' mouths. While Limpet might have animated my sense of vulnerability: given me an access to my bodily contingency, Gino's influence helped nudge my fear into selfishness.

One afternoon, there was an incident that changed things. I was unpacking crates when I heard my name called out. Someone was out front, looking for me. When I emerged from behind the stack, all I saw was a flash of red nylon before he was upon me, blows raining down.

In another moment they stopped. I was being dragged backwards, Malik's arms under my armpits. As I righted myself on my elbows I saw Gino, straddling the prone red snowsuit, his arms swinging huge alternating arcs: tireless, pneumatic. Eventually someone pulled him off, but not before he whispered some words in the man's ear and spat in his bloodied face. Gino walked past us, pausing to wipe his hands on my snowsuit. 'Don't mention it,' he said. And what he meant was: make sure I never have to.

We found out later that someone had witnessed the killing in London Fields, had been combing a house of their own.

The body lay in the snow until his brother went looking for him. When he found him, he set out to find who had done it. This witness had traded our names for a gallon of diesel.

That man, the brother of the man I had killed, lay in front of me, his chest heaving, his nose streaming. He staggered to his feet and pushed his way through the startled crowd of people shocked immobile by the sudden violence.

For the next few weeks, I lived in a state of heightened anxiety. Malik and I went everywhere together, watching each other's backs, jumping at every shadow, every thump fall of windblown snow. But as the weeks went on, and nothing else happened, I began to relax. A notion began to develop that Gino had taken it upon himself to settle the matter, once and for all. This was a question he held over me, because I never had the courage to ask.

Gino had an instinct for dominance, for finding the particular lever that circumstances have required. The lever that he had over me was a question with which I was tortured: how far did this safety extend, and for how long?

I hadn't imagined that the answer would come in St Paul's churchyard.

Sam pauses inside the porch of the cathedral and rubs the pamphlet between his thumb and forefinger. 'Still warm from a photocopier.' He holds it up to his nose and sniffs. 'Heaven.'

As we move through the entrance towards the nave the lilting sound of a single woman's voice, singing some kind of liturgy in Latin, echoes towards us along with a strong smell of incense.

The context switch is so complete that it feels impossible that the man I spotted outside could have followed me in here. Hanging from the aisles, on either side of the nave, are huge woven tapestries. I try to dismiss my anxiety and paranoia, to put aside the memories the feelings summoned. This is what I have come to see.

The grandeur is so totally at odds with the scene in

Haggerston, that day we made the trip to All Saints, just as I hoped. I've seen versions of these visions on the feeds. Hildegard's visions. Bizarre concoctions in flat perspective, of angels engulfed in geometric flames; a floating head radiating wings buttressed by ramparts; a nun sketching on a wax tablet, fingers of fire seeming to emerge from her eyes, pooling above her on the domed ceiling. Here they are reproduced in breathtaking scale, each twenty to thirty feet across, woven in bright and shining stitch, so lustrous in the candlelight and incense smoke that for a moment I freeze in place.

On first glance, they seem chaotic and esoteric – familiar shapes interrupted by obscure growths and projections. But to anyone who has lived alongside the feeds since the Thaw, constantly bombarded by aura of every conceivable shade and stripe, the eye very quickly strips away the medieval estrangement, the changes in representation wrought across a thousand years, to see the visions for what they are. Divine weather. Bible stories rewritten, rewired by misfiring synapses.

I replay my own aura from the previous night. The writhing fortifications of light, stroked by spectra, fill the top right-hand side of my vision. Fighting nausea, summoned by the sense memory – the sweet scent of incense suddenly sickly – I turn to the vision of the floating head. I line up the playback of my own vision with the fortifications falling away from the head, under the wings. They are almost identical.

I feel my heart in my throat – a bewildering sense of recognition crossing centuries. Isn't this what I've wanted, a way to feel continuous? I understand, now, the power they hold in tracing an experience that my mind – my whole body – has been fighting to supress since last night. The feeling is a version of awe: fear and amazement commingling as the pleasure of being seen conflicts with a terror that the reflection might go beyond summoning the vision that it replicates, to bring on all of the other bodily disorder that went along with it.

In this aversion, I feel myself groping at the edges of something: what this new experience might mean.

A hand appears in front of my face, Sam's. I suspend the aura overlay and wave him away.

There's a strand of migraineurs who have sought to historicise their condition, to collect precedents to build a case that the attacks are the culmination and realisation of a divine plan.

The idea being that the epidemic of migraine is the overture to the rapture. Those suffering from visions are being offered a preview of the day of judgement, when God and his host of angels will return, to divide the damned from the saved. The five-year Freeze represents the culmination of man's folly. The Thaw is the opening move in our demise.

It isn't hard to guess who, between the sick and the well, are destined to be saved in this interpretation. It was this kind of messianic thinking that turned me off in the past, but now that I have touched the feeling behind it, I feel suddenly more charitable.

Hildegard has become a figure to organise around, for these migraineurs. She was a medieval nun. A member of the Benedictine Order at the turn of the first millennium in Germany, she experienced a series of visions which she interpreted as messages from God.

Commanded by these visions, she broke away from the order and set up a new community. Here she set down her visions and illustrated them by sketching what she had seen onto a wax tablet, creating tableaux which were illuminated by the nuns in her community into the images which were now woven into the tapestries hanging all around us.

I learned all of this scrolling the feeds one night at your flat, while watching you work.

I recognise the soaring arpeggios that the sole chorister is singing as one of the monophonic chants composed by Hildegard, which now accompany all of the clips posted on the feeds by her followers. She was a polymath. Aside from being a mystic, she was also a herbalist, a philosopher and a composer. Her followers took a holistic approach to positioning themselves as her spiritual heirs.

A second voice joins the first, a cross melody. Hildegard's compositions have been adapted to fit the theory that listening to binaural music, two tones of close but slightly distinct frequencies, encourages the mind to synthesise them into a third – and that this synthesis in turn supports the synchronisation of activity across the whole brain through a process called entrainment, counteracting the disorder caused by migraine. The church has been quick to add biohacking to its devotions. It's popular on the feeds with migraineurs adding viral binaural tracks to their clips, accompanied by whispered affirmations. Full sensory ASMR.

It isn't until I reach the dome that I spot the singers – high up above us in the whispering galley, leaning against the balustrade. People are fanning out around us, taking seats.

Sam pauses, circling, looking down at his feet. Below us, directly under the apex of the dome, is the most famous of all of Hildegard's visions. The marble floor has been whitewashed and painted over with a giant blue egg, speckled with golden stars and surrounded by two layers: the first, night black and filled with small cairns of hailstones from which issue red forking lightning; the second, a golden mane, each hair a blade of red-rimmed fire.

At the tip of the fiery mane is the sun and, below this, separated by two smaller celestial bodies – perhaps Mercury and Venus – is the moon, and finally Earth.

Hildegard's version of Earth is the strangest part of the whole thing. So accustomed are we to the images taken from space, showing our world suspended, pristine and shining in hard vacuum, that to encounter a reckoning which predates the moment when our perspective achieved escape velocity is unnerving.

Her earth is bodily: a site of currents and eruptions. The organic blues, greens and violet hues rubbing up against and intersecting one another, a place perceived from within, by experience, rather than from without by representation.

I pace the edge of the egg, placing my feet carefully one after the other inside the giant flaming hairs at the edge of Hildegard's universe. Lulled into a receptive trance by the music. I feel, for a moment, the persuasiveness of this huge volume of space.

A murmur and a sudden hush. Movement up ahead in the quire. Something is about to begin, so I come to my senses sufficiently to find a seat.

The singing comes quite suddenly to a halt, the final note lingering in the air for a moment before a full-throated choir, singing a liturgy, rises in its place.

To the right of the quire the procession emerges and everyone begins to get to their feet. Sam shakes his head, chuckling to himself at the eagerness of those around him. He splutters as I drag him to his feet.

Three women in white silk, stitched with motifs from Hildegard's aura – stars at the elbows, golden flames winding around the bell sleeves girding their forearms. On their heads they wear delicate crowns of gold. Out in front: two young girls, one bearing a cross and another swinging a censor of incense.

The three women take their places in front of the quire and bow their heads. When the voices of the choir fall silent, one of them steps forward, a book open in her hands.

'First vision. The Iron Mountain.'

She pauses as the people around me began to reorientate themselves, craning to the left to face the north aisle, tapping at their temples. The woman reads on:

'I saw the likeness of a great mountain the colour of iron, and on it sat a figure in great brightness, so bright that it dazzled my eyes.'

I follow the attention of the crowd towards a tapestry, the first in the series as you enter the nave. It shows God – winged and robed in red and gold – sitting atop a mountain pocked with windows, a pair of forlorn and devout figures staring out of each one. From the hem of the figure's robe issues a golden strip of cloth, flowing down the side of the mountain, terminating at the neck of an otherwise headless figure, its hands raised in supplication. To the right of this figure is another, covered all over with eyes.

What is so particularly enthralling about this tapestry, among the embarrassment of strangeness that decks the aisles of the chamber? I turn to Sam, but he just pouts and shrugs. Experimentally, I initiate my implant and turn back to the tapestry.

At first, it seems that nothing has changed, but then the golden figure beats its wings. I blink, and it beats its wings again, lifting its head to the heavens. I gasp.

'What?' Sam stage whispers. 'What is it? What can you see?'

I shush and wave him away. The nun continues.

'And suddenly the man seated on the mountain called out in a loud and penetrating voice and said . . .'

The beating of the figure's wings intensifies. I realise that, somehow, I can hear it. A real sound, unaugmented, from somewhere, up in the gallery, the distinctive thumping sound echoes down to us.

'Can you hear that?' Sam says. 'What is . . .'

But the sound of his voice is lost in the exclamations of everyone surrounding us as the golden-winged figure rises from the tapestry and breaks away across the nave towards the dome, the heads of the figures in the windows cut into the mountain following its flight path.

It comes to a stop above the three nuns, who hold their arms wide. Turning its head left and right, it opens its mouth and from someplace above it in the whispering gallery a booming voice issues, which sounds in the bones of my chest:

Human creature in your weakness, in the dust and ashes of the earth! Cry out and speak of the entry to lasting salvation . . .

I turn off my implant and the golden figure disappears. The stunned faces of the people around me tell their own story: I have never seen the Neurals used this way. People start falling to their knees, prostrating themselves as the voice continues.

For you do not receive this profound and penetrating discernment from a human being. Rather, you receive it from the heavenly and awe-inspiring Judge on high.

The voices of the choir rise to meet the fading echo of the angel's words. It is vivid. In the sense that it is alive. It shifts with the rhythm of my heart or, perhaps, it was the other way around. This attunement is too much. My tongue feels thick and tears are welling. I am struck again by the question of whether this is how it will always feel, in the days after a storm. Will I always leave my body to return to one that snags in unexpected places in time's flow, where before it had drifted serenely on? Existing, for a moment, in this porous state of depersonalisation (is this, still, part of the migraine?) between the two states I could perceive the invisible lie that I had been living, one that anchored the person that I thought I was: that I haven't been living in my body at all.

From this vantage, as I observe the undulating feeling of ecstatic serenity flooding my chest, I feel it begin to sour. It is like that fulcrum moment in a dream when you realise you are falling through space or driving a car with no steering wheel. I begin to panic.

Out of the corner of my eye, I see something familiar: is it that face again? The brother? But when I rise up and swivel, turning to catch hold of it fully, I am met with the same rows of curved backs, or oblivious, beatific faces.

There is an aspect of the face I seek in each – arch of the brow, curl of the lip – a serpentine semblance which slips further away the more I seek it. I turn back and in the stretch of the nun's arms the fall of my own – that morning by London Fields – intrudes.

I stagger towards the aisle, gasping for breath, tripping over supplicated forms separating me from safety.

I can hear Sam calling my name behind me in a stage whisper. Blows are striking my legs. I have to get out.

Do you remember how, during the Freeze, there was a fashion for the horrible in the imaginary?

Everyone was competing to outdo one another. Everything was horrible. Incest, disinterment, disembowelment, death, destruction and misery. Anything unpleasant, unsavoury, unsanitary or unnatural that could be inflicted on a body was wrung out for every last drop of existential horror. As though by describing the very worst that could happen, it might somehow be prevented.

There was that period of time when the most popular content – apart from porn, always the first use of a new technology – were clips capturing the moment of a person's death.

The first time I came upon one, it took me unawares as I was scrolling through the feeds. A pursuit, from the perspective of the pursued – heavy breathing, a blur of visuals as the subject cast their eyes desperately around, and then a sudden blast in the haptics, a burning sensation that travelled up my spine. A masked figure stepped into the centre of the field, holding a bloodied knife, before the clip came to an abrupt end.

The anonymous gangs who would run people down, kill them, pull the data of their final moments from their implants and then upload it to the feeds, were probably still among us. They were probably working alongside us at the farms, waving to us in the street.

Those clips were the apogee of the nihilism that characterised the worst moments of the Freeze. We had never been more closely networked, and we had never been more alone.

When the Thaw arrived, with the migraines and the turn away from catastrophising on the feeds towards the aurashows, that slogan arrived too – the one sprayed on the paving stones of St Paul's churchyard.

Solidarity not charity. Now we had a new principle to organise around. It was an absolute, something non-negotiable. It couldn't be reasoned with or cajoled. It couldn't be turned to a purpose, or trained to obedience.

The principle was pain. Even those that were spared its physical and spiritual effects were subject to its social ones. When it arrived, the world stopped, and when it lifted the world resumed its spin.

After all, those of us who didn't suffer from the pain – the able-bodied among us – stood to benefit most from the truce that it had brought about: the prohibition, above all else, to ask the question that might bring the whole edifice down.

How did you survive?

Without asking it directly, you and I were feeling our way around the edges of this question. I've gone back over these conversations in my mind a thousand times, trying to find any openings – ones that I missed.

A few days after the day at All Saints, which I had been apologising so profusely for, you banned me from mentioning it, we had one of these conversations.

'You like that I don't get migraines, don't you?' I asked.

You considered me, took my face in your cupped hand. 'I suppose I do.'

'Why, though?'

'Hmm,' you said, leaning in to kiss my cheek.

'It bothers me, for some reason. That it's the thing that attracted you to me.'

'The grand and terrible mystery of heterosexuality,' you said, laughing.

'I'm sorry that I got kind of sucked in.' You gave me a warning look. 'I'm not bringing it up again, it's just part of me wants . . . I don't know.' I paused, tried again. 'All that time, with Malik. Our self-reliance was the thing. It was at the heart of our friendship. And now . . .'

You put your head to my chest and said, in a quieter voice: 'Do you think that any of this could have happened, though, if not for the headaches?'

'Any of this?' I pulled back, stung. 'You and me?'

'No, no,' you said quickly. 'The co-ops, the farms. Everyone finally . . .' You paused, looking for the right words. 'Finally admitting that there is enough space for everyone else.'

I could feel your heartbeat, through your shirt, and my heart beating in your ear. An intrusion: the weight of the crowbar in my hand, a metallic taste, the beat of my heart in my tongue. I pushed it away.

'I don't know,' I said.

'There will always be men who feel like the world owes them something. Always have been. If the end of civilisation won't satisfy their perverted sense of justice then nothing will.'

'Did you ever see a therapist?' I asked.

'That's your response!'

I laughed, a little too loud – grateful for the shifting tension, the sense that a course had been charted back to safer ground. 'I don't mean it like that, I just mean: did you ever buy into the theory?'

Another one. Another attempt to ignore the obvious cause and effect. The theory that the headaches were post-traumatic – that spending five years re-adjusting to an ice age that ended as abruptly as it began had led to an outbreak of some kind of collective hysteria, something like the dancing manias that struck in villages around Europe in the middle ages in the wake of the Black Death, when whole communities would dance under the spell of some unknown hypnotic impulse until they collapsed with exhaustion.

There *had* been a sudden surge in demand for therapy. Most of the analysts and psychotherapists had left when the weather changed, so quacks with two-week certificates offering cognitive behavioural therapy, augmented by haptic feedback, became impossible to avoid on the feeds.

'Whenever a woman gets ill, it's always their feelings that are to blame.'

'Come on, Luna.' I grinned. 'You're being hysterical.'

You lashed out at my chest and I caught your wrist in my

hand. You slipped your hand under my T-shirt. Always the first escape route from any playful friction that threatened to sour – skin on skin. I had been so starved of intimacy, still felt such hopeless gratitude for its power to find the shortest line between two points, that I was an ever-willing accomplice in the diversion.

*

A few days later, we spoke again, dancing around the question. We started with that clouded arc of time that stretched between when we had known each other at school and then when we met again, as adults.

'Let's play "where were you when",' you said, one night, when we were cooking.

'OK,' I said. 'Where do we start?'

I had been in my second year, studying politics at Goldsmith's, when the snow began to fall. I loved it, though not quite enough to move south of the river. It was the perfect atmosphere for agonising over who was to blame. But that wasn't what we alighted on first.

'Trump?' you said. 'What were you doing when he got elected?'

'That's an easy one. He ruined my birthday. It happened the day before.'

'Just realised, I never asked you: when is your birthday?' You looked furtively over your shoulder at me, moving courgettes around in the frying pan. 'I haven't missed it, have I?'

'No, you haven't missed it. November.'

'Scorpio?'

'Yes. Is that bad? I've never figured it out.'

'We could do your chart. Your rising sign is important, too. I'm a Leo.'

'Luna the lion.'

You gave a little growl, then paused, your eyes going up to the ceiling. 'I stayed up and watched the coverage all night. The guy with the magic board going county by county.'

'It felt like the end of something.' I wrapped my arms around your waist and felt the faint warmth from the stove on my fingers.

You leaned into me. 'Or the beginning of something, I guess.'

'Everyone was so fucking grim at my birthday drinks,' I said. 'Like someone had died. Who could have imagined how much worse things could get?'

You pulled away from me, began spooning the food out into bowls. You were silent for a moment, dressing our food with parsley that I had brought from the farm. 'Let's look at it this way: what do you miss?'

I thought about it. 'Bagels.'

'What about the bread I make?'

'From the supermarket. The sesame ones. And chocolate. I mean shit chocolate: Dairy Milk and Mars bars.'

'I miss Dairy Milk when I get my period.'

'What else?'

'My life is better, now, I think.' You handed me a bowl. 'In a lot of ways, I think, it's better.'

'What about the headaches?'

'The headaches I had before. And before, they didn't mean anything.'

'What, you've always had migraines? They didn't start with the Thaw?'

You laughed. 'Does that ruin the mystique? Why do you think I was so quick to see what they could be? On the feeds?'

I did feel strangely disappointed. As though you'd had a head start. Perhaps that was something that we'd share now though, that we're both slightly out of step – with your migraines coming early, and mine coming late.

I covered this disappointment by looping back. 'Bagels, though?'

'Sure, I miss bagels. And the idea . . .' You paused, chewing thoughtfully. 'What they represent I suppose.'

'And what do bagels represent to you?'

'You know what I mean,' you said, putting down your bowl in frustration. 'I feel like living in a city, where everything was just brought in and neatly packaged and on the shelves, you were part of this bigger, invisible thing.'

'You mean . . . society?'

You rolled her eyes at me. 'I'm talking about safety. The assumption of safety that being able to just buy stuff gave you. That all the complexity involved was sealed away, but somehow near. There was an invisible chain running through things.'

'I was very anxious,' I said. 'I feel less anxious now.'

'Less anxious, less safe.' You finished your meal and put down your bowl, placing a hand on my forearm. 'Do you know what I mean though?'

'I think so. The world was like an iPhone. All the complexity was sealed away.'

'I guess?'

'At least, now,' I said, 'we know who that seeming simplicity was for. Because it wasn't for us.'

'You were the one who said you missed supermarket bagels.'

'There were some consolations. Where were you, then? When it started to snow.'

You looked away. 'I was here.'

This is where I should have asked why you never came to Haggerston station during the Freeze. Why you never turned up to collect food or fuel. But instead, I asked: 'When did your parents leave?'

'Almost immediately. They cashed in on what they could and rented a place in northern Spain.'

'Why didn't you go with them?'

You sighed. 'I thought they were being hysterical. And then, when it gradually became clear to everyone that they were right, I was too proud. By the time I realised that I should have been with them because, once their money ran out, it was obviously going to be them that needed me, they were in one of the camps. By that point . . .'

'Closed.'

'Yep.' You leaned back against the counter and took a deep breath, chin to chest, visibly drawing brightness back to yourself, out of the air, by a force of will. You smiled at me and I smiled gamely back, waiting for the crease of your brow that would accompany your inevitable reply: 'What about your parents?'

'My dad wasn't really in the picture. My mum left, too, when the snow started. Early doors. I don't know where she is either but I imagine . . . Well, I try not to imagine.'

'Yeh . . .' You squeezed my arm.

'Not really a "no news is good news" kind of a situation. You know, she always used to tell me stories about living in squats. Late '70s and early '80s, she lived in one of those big houses over by London Fields, on Lansdowne Drive, with a load of artists and writers. It would give her this faraway look. She was always a little bitter she didn't stick around long enough. We would occasionally run into some of the people she'd lived with who had stayed in those houses long enough that they came to own them.' I sighed. 'If she had stuck around. She'd love all this. Live where you like. Eat what you grow. Just like the good old days.'

'There's always a chance,' you said. 'That they'll come back.'

'It's the hope that kills you,' I said. Your face fell. I realised that you were speaking more, in that moment, for yourself than for me.

What I really missed, and it had taken me a long time to figure this out, was the guarantee of forgiveness that my mum had always offered me. It wasn't something I realised I had from her, this guarantee, until it was gone, into the silence of her disappearance. Part of me knew, before – was reassured of the fact – that whatever I did, whoever I became, she would have forgiven me. Automatically. Without question. Which is why I doubly regret not telling her what happened, about what I did.

But how to say that, without foregrounding its obvious self-ishness. How to summon, then, the memory of her without recalling with it what I strove each day to forget.

'I miss her,' I said, searching for the pivot point. 'More than bagels.'

You released your held breath, the held thought. 'More than bagels. I miss my parents more than bagels.'

'But not more than Dairy Milk?'

You laughed. 'You always do that.'

'What?'

'Find a callback. A safe one. Whenever I try and steer a conversation onto the rocks. Make something happen.'

'Sorry,' I said. 'I know. I want to, you know, diffuse the tension. I don't know why. It's just this stupid impulse.'

'Same impulse as telling your stories.'

'How do you mean?' I asked, curiosity tipping the scales on my caution.

'To make things safe. Hold them in place. Wrap them in a little invention.'

'Give me an example.'

'The woman and the sunglasses?'

'So, what am I wrapping in invention there?'

'Let me ask you this,' you said, leaning into me. 'How do you see yourself?'

'That's a little broad.'

'OK,' you said, pouting a little, thoughtfully. 'How about this. Are you the same guy, as before? Do you see yourself the same way as you did, before . . .' you gestured wildly with your arms, encompassing the room, encompassing the world, 'before all this?'

Before I could stop myself, I said: 'With you, I do. I guess, you make me feel . . . with you I suppose I do.'

You beamed. 'I suppose I do too.'

I stumble down the steps of St Paul's, gasping for air.

I feel skinless, like a segment of orange wetly gleaming. Sam is at my heels saying something, but I can't make out the words, which seem both distant and too loud – a megaphone with the gain turned all the way up. I feel the noise in my teeth, can taste the light on my tongue.

I have had panic attacks before, but not since before the Freeze. I have associated them in my mind, up to this point, with the frenetic pace that characterised life then. I think back to our conversation in your kitchen. I want to ask you whether you've always lived with this fear of bringing on a migraine. Whether it has a different strain, for you, than all of the other fears we've lived alongside since it began to snow.

'Wait.' A hand on my shoulder. 'Ellis, just wait.'

I turn and Sam is doubled over, sweat darkening the armpits of his filthy seersucker suit. The dome looks squat and sinister behind his head, a bone-gleam against the high clouds. A drone following a pre-programmed pattern circles above and the churchyard feels half-abandoned, a stark contrast to the thrum that greeted us on arrival.

I press my index finger into the tender sheet of muscle at my temple and try to slow my breathing. As air inflates my lungs pain gathers, hot and fibrous, under my finger. Was this some kind of after-shock?

'What the fuck is wrong with you?' Sam pants.

'Is it always like this?' I say. 'The day after.'

'Like what?'

'Mad. I've gone mad.'

Sam straightens up, looks me up and down. 'What's more terrifying than death?'

'I don't know, dying?'

'Just this: knowing that everyone else – every single person – has an inner life as rich and varied as our own.'

Despite myself, I laugh. 'I don't know, not everyone has as much main character energy as you.'

Sam looks at me blankly. Then abruptly he walks away across the churchyard. 'It doesn't help to talk about it. Everyone thinks that they have a way to stop it, but they don't. It's the climate. It's just something to be endured.'

'That's comforting, thanks.' It's magical thinking to be convinced that you can talk your way out of a migraine, but it is also madness to think that talking about it brings it on. I want to reject this aversion. If this is to bring me closer to you, it has to be something that I can grasp.

The migraine stole away my language. Whenever I think about it, I can only re-experience it. There has to be a way of describing it, without being drawn into the hole it has opened up. I feel a new understanding of the appeal of the aurashows on the feeds. They offer something outside of language that allows you to be with the experience, safely: disembodied yet not depersonalised; with the beauty but at a remove from the horror. In St Paul's I felt, for a few moments, too close to reliving the real thing.

'When you had your first one,' I say, 'did you feel like there was a crack? Suddenly. In everything?'

Sam laughs. 'Such drama,' he says, and then pauses for a moment. 'What was it that you did, exactly, to make this girl run halfway across London to get away from you?'

He has caught me off guard. 'I pushed her away. I thought I could forget my past by pretending that she didn't have one.'

'Not ready to let the light in.'

'Yeh, something like that.'

'I had my first migraine when I was twelve,' Sam says. 'My parents thought I was on drugs.'

'Feel like there's another story to be told there.'

'One for another day. No one believes children. Or the sick. Or women. But still, I never mistook the headaches for some kind of revelation.'

'Why do you say that?

'Isn't that what you've been chasing around after? All day?'

Without my noticing we have turned back on ourselves, bending a course back towards the city. Behind us, a church that had been made over into a coffee shop – long abandoned – or so I surmised by the sign that has fallen to hang slantwise across the doorway. The bells of St Paul's start to ring. I close my eyes and picture the scene from above: the pilgrims streaming into the churchyard. In this vision, they all pause as one, and gaze upwards. They all have the same face. The brother's face. I open my eyes.

'Come on,' I say. 'Let's go over Southwark Bridge. I could do with a break from the crowds.'

We are drawn, by the gradient, down into the remains of a tiny park, which steps in terraces down towards the river.

'There were Roman baths here,' Sam says, pointing to a section of crumbling masonry in the park's boundary wall, marked out by colour and age. 'At one time, even a vineyard. When the snow first melted and the storms started, the night after one hit I began going on long walks.'

How many people, like me, like Sam, are tracing their own private geographies over the scarred face of the city? How many lonely pilgrim trails are stamped into the cracked tarmac each night?

'I'd make a circuit of the Roman walls. It's all there. The roads are ramparts. Start out where Bishopsgate meets London Wall and follow clockwise to Aldgate and then on to the Tower. Follow the river along Thames Street, up Blackfriars Lane, past the Old Bailey – where I did jury service, in the days before all this, and was shown by a bailiff the cell in the basement of the courts where condemned men would be kept, when it was still a prison, from which led a path straight to the gallows. Finally, I'd cut along Newgate back up to London Wall and follow it back to where I'd started.'

By now we have reached the bottom of the park and come out onto Upper Thames Street, running parallel to the river, previously hidden by the looming office blocks that rise up on either side. The street is deserted: eerie after the press of people, sound and sensation we have so recently fled. Sam takes the maps from his pocket, leafing through them.

A movement. A shadow falling against one of the panes of unbroken glass. But when I look back, there is nothing. I shake my head to clear it. Sam doesn't seem to have noticed anything, lost in his reverie.

'I wanted to reassure myself,' he says, 'that the place that the snow had buried was still there. Like the Roman city, still here in the remnants: the names and the old shapes. After I got bored of following the ghost of the walls, I began walking in concentric circles towards the centre. People hadn't begun finding their way back, yet. In the pissing rain, at the shutters of a shop where I had bought a suit for a friend's wedding, I found my way back. At a corner where I'd nearly been clattered by a black cab, where I'd abandoned my bike in the middle of the road to scream myself purple from the fierce adrenaline. Under the sign of a pub where I'd received the call that my grandma had died. It all floated back up, from under the cracked paving.'

In the oppressive atmosphere of the empty and quiet street, there is a hypnotic rhythm to Sam's words, accruing against the thin film of exhaustion which I haven't been able to pierce all day. In a place like this, replete with incidental artefacts, how did I ever think it would be possible to escape my own past?

We have reached the bridge, Sam still ahead of me, walking a little faster. As the buildings give way to the river a wind catches my jacket and sets it flapping. Off to the left, the Shard shines in the sunlight. To the right, the crumbling brick chimney of the Tate. The familiarity of the buildings ranged against the sky, and the sense of the enclosure from the wind in my ears reassures me.

I pull my jacket around myself and close my eyes, my eager lungs sucking in the mud-scoured air. I pause to give myself a moment to let these feelings wash over me.

Unlike Sam, I haven't wanted to be continuous. Too much of the time, I've wanted to be erased. Under this pressure it's not so surprising that, with you, I began to fail to recognise myself.

There is a hand on my shoulder, a tugging sensation I register before I open my eyes to see Sam turning towards me, before I watch the shock unfold itself across his face. I feel relief. A certain resignation.

It is all automatic. My movements and the feelings, rote. I stand outside myself and watch it all happening again, as though for the first time.

The killing blow is a re-inscription of the first. The fear that has been stalking me all day is not a repeat of the migraine, but a repeat of my violence.

I swing my elbow backwards and meet the soft tissue of a solar plexus, before dropping to one knee to pull the knife from my boot and press from the balls of my feet, upwards, to meet the torso as it doubles over towards me, drawn – by my blow – into that reflex to protect its soft centre, to instead invite the blade I hold, upwards, in my fist to pierce nylon, cotton and finally, with sickening ease, yielding flesh.

I feel the hot welt of breath in the shell of my ear as I turn to face the lights, fast fading on an exhaled breath, of those eyes that have followed us all day.

I feel a familiar sinking, a homely shame, as I come back to myself. I straighten and the man is slumped hard against me, his face a picture of dismayed surprise as he slides down to the ground. I don't need to look to see who it is. I knew in the instant I felt the hand on my shoulder, as though it reached out across time rather than space. The brother that had fled; the brother that had bound me to Gino.

Because of course he came back. Of course, the only way for it to end was by my hand, or his. Sam is right: all day I have been seeking a revelation, something transcendent that will allow me to avoid a disclosure.

The other man, the one I don't recognise, had been tussling with Sam. Noticing his fallen companion, the knife in my hand, he throws up his hands and flees back towards the city.

Sam is upon me, turning my hands in his own, looking for the source of the blood that slicks them. He pats my chest, my arms.

'Not mine,' I say, finally. A crack in my voice, but no light.

Luna, the simple answer to that unutterable question that we couldn't ask one another, the one that stood between us, was always crouched in the raw memory of my nerves. All of which is to say I survived because others did not.

Sam nods, and we run into the wind towards Southwark.

I know that this account that I have been giving of myself might seem strangely distanced.

Before last night's migraine attack, when all my knowledge of them came from simulacra from the implant, when I thought of migraine I always thought of the Hollywood symptoms first: lights, pain, nausea – the neurological patina of the new world we've created in its image.

Depersonalisation is less common, but I found it to be the most profound part of the experience. As I drifted outside myself, I felt – for the first time in a long time – that I was able to see myself, as I really am.

So I thought: why couldn't that be a strategy? Go away from myself to come back. If I can get outside of myself, outside of us, I might also make myself more legible to you.

And so I'll continue, attempting to be impersonal, dispassionate. Let me try to explain, where I began to lose my way with us. The night I came home, drunk, after a session with Malik at the Welly.

Malik and I had been drinking there since we'd split the cost of a fake ID (went with Malik's photo, more convincing facial hair) so we could drink pints in plastic in the sun on the patch of grass outside. Ever since – birthdays, break-ups, north London derbies, celebrating getting a job, celebrating quitting a job – it had been our place. We loved it: a proper boozer, with a semi-circular dark-wood bar under strip lights. No food. A faded print of the Duke himself hanging above the pool table.

I had been avoiding him, nursing a sense of grievance since the day at the church. Eventually, it needed an outlet. One afternoon, I sought him out, where I knew he could be found. I sat down next to him on a bench outside; he looked half-cut already.

'I thought you had disappeared,' he said. 'Or fucking died.'

'So, you did miss me,' I said.

'Simp.' He smiled.

'You made me look like a knob.'

'From Sigma to simp.' He held up his hands, one after the other, as though he was putting it up in lights.

I could feel my anger rising and spiralling out of my grip. 'What is that from? The "When's It Going to Be Our Turn" manifesto?'

He looked genuinely taken aback. 'Straight into it? Won't even let me wet your whistle?'

'Come on, admit it. You wanted to make me look like a daft cunt, in front of Luna.'

'We were just having a laugh, no? Remember that? Remember

having a laugh?' He put his arm around my shoulder, squeezing. I could feel the tension in my teeth and my spine. 'Come on, I'll get a freshener. Have a couple of jars. You can tell me all about what a prick I am. I'll grab my notebook.'

Before I met you, I was there most nights with Malik and a revolving cast of Hackney survivors – even rota'd myself in for a couple of evenings a week at one point, to wage my drinking for the rest of the week. Before his parents left, Malik had hidden his drinking from them out of respect. No such need now. The place had been abandoned during the Freeze but when we came to recolonise it the baize on the pool table had somehow survived (the landlord had always been careful with it). We spent months attempting to recreate the perfect pint of Guinness from memory, with liquid nitrogen pilfered from Homerton Hospital's derelict lab and barley roasted in a gas oven in the back of the pub. Everyone had something to forget and sitting outside, with a pint during the golden hour when the sun hit the whitewashed frontage of the pub, you could imagine for a moment that nothing had ever changed.

Malik arrived with the pints. As soon as he put them down, he took out his latest product.

He'd moved on from Tiger Balm and food colouring and managed to hook up with another chemist, some west London hippy Oxbridge type who had been experimenting with ethers and claimed to have found a way of delivering opiates through the skin. Apparently, it didn't have the habit-forming problems that you got with Oxy.

'And you want me to give this shit to my girlfriend?'

'You told me she liked the other one, no?'

'And once she's hooked you're going to ... what, exactly?

Cuckoo the flat? Start launching drones from the roof of the tower? Like the fucking Wicked Witch of the West?'

'Good grief, Ellis. What did you have on your cornflakes this morning?' He took a sip from his pint. 'Fuck are you to judge me, anyway?'

I could feel the conversation slipping like rope through my hands. I paused to take a sip from my beer, to collect myself. I wanted him to take the thing between you and me seriously. I tried to find the right words. Malik shifted in his seat. This wasn't the tenor that our conversations usually took.

'Look,' he said, before I could say anything else. 'I didn't want to say anything. Really, I didn't. I know you're really keen on her. And honestly, she's been good for you. This anger ... it's, well, it's something. It's better than the Eeyore act that you had going on before.'

'Eeyore act?'

'The cloud you've been living under. Ever since the Thaw.'

'It's hard to adjust.'

'I know, it's hard on everyone.'

'What is it? If you've got something to say to me, just say it.'

'I let him know – Gobber, Gino, whatever we're going to call him – that you were going to be there. You and Luna'.

'Why?'

'I thought it might, I don't know ... bring things to a head.'

'Why do you want to bring him back into our lives? He's a hypocrite. Says hateful things with a smile on his face so that if anyone calls him out on it, he can claim it's all just a big joke.'

'Oh, *he's* a hypocrite.'

'And the joke is: if you're not like us, then fuck you. That's the joke. That's all it is.'

'So there's nothing hypocritical about you . . .'

'What?' I said.

He finished his beer. 'Nothing hypocritical about her, acting all high and fucking mighty when . . .'

'When what?'

He stood. 'No, look, forget about it. Shouldn't have . . .' He trailed off and held out his hand. 'Do you want to have another one?'

I looked at my glass, also empty. My mouth dry. 'Come on. Out with it. What is it you've got to say to me about Luna.'

Malik sighed, shifted from one foot to the other. 'I should have left it, it just sticks in my craw when, through all of it, she was with Gino.' He pauses. 'Living with him.'

My skin began to tingle, and my breath caught in my throat. My body indexing certain experiences as I fought their reinscription, shaking my head to push them away.

'I mean, what does it matter who she was with. How do you know, anyway?' I said, watching myself from above.

He leaned over and tugged gently at the pint glass I had wrapped my hands around. 'I'll get us another.'

Since the Thaw, in an attempt to dispel the cloud that Malik had described, before I met you, when I wasn't at the Welly I spent evenings seeking out luminosity in crises throughout history: stories of heroism and selflessness in the wake of fires and floods, earthquakes and terrorist attacks. I made a collection of them: a paraplegic man who was carried down sixty-three flights of the North Tower by ten of his co-workers, working in relay, the morning the planes struck the Twin Towers; a woman who started a soup kitchen with one can to drink from and one pie plate to eat from in the Golden Gate Park in the wake of the

San Francisco earthquake. Ordinary people doing extraordinary things but also extraordinary people doing ordinary things. I cached the video of Obama singing 'Amazing Grace' at a funeral after the Charleston shootings, before reciting the names of all the people who had been killed, declaring, in turn, that they had 'found that Grace'. In my weaker moments, I'd watch it on a loop, bathing in that upswell sentimentality channelled by his unhinged charisma until the inevitable tears swelled as a kind of relief, a kind of revelation.

I told myself that all of this was to forget people like Gino, opportunists who lack this first instinct to move together – who turn against this tide of good will and walk in the opposite direction. The kind of people who rush back into the burning building, back up the stairs past the stranded paraplegic to snatch the abandoned wallets from people's desks. I thought that this torrent of sentimentality was the way out, until I met you. Now it seems sociopathic. Nostalgia is a cheap stand-in for memory. And it's clear that I wasn't doing it to forget about him, but to forget that I was like him.

Without realising, I had begun to itch at the patches of scarred skin at my wrists and ankles. I pressed my palms against the rising heat in my wrists and then pulled the cuffs of my jumper over my hands, folding my fingers into fists against the temptation.

Malik reappeared looking sheepish and placed the pints on the table in front of us. As he sipped I could feel his sidelong glances, waiting to see whether I would speak.

'Knew I shouldn't have said anything.'

'Where did this rumour come from?'

'It's not a rumour. One of the guys that we used to run with at the aid station heard you'd hooked up with Luna. We've all been messaging about this transformation Gino has undergone . . .'

I paused, but Malik didn't say anything. Left the silence for me to fill. 'Who cares who she was with before me? I'm not that guy. Don't want to be that jealous guy.'

'I know, you're right.'

'Everyone's got a history.'

'We do, we all do.'

We sat and drank our pints in silence; the sun had dropped behind high clouds on the horizon and I rubbed my hands together against the cold. A pleasant numbness was arriving into my irritated skin. I had that familiar sensation of a casual drink turning into a session; the hardening of conversation from something pliant and branching into something circular. Evenings spent guessing the population of European capitals – before, after. Naming every brand of crisp that we could no longer get our hands on. Every Premier League top scorer, starting in 1992. The safety of boring familiarity.

I wanted to resist it, to catch a handhold.

'Do you remember the foxes?' I said. 'The tame ones?'

'Landlady used to feed them.'

'Fried chicken.'

'Yeh, closing time. Right out of her hand.'

'Used to freak me out a little to be honest, how unafraid they were.'

'Wasn't there a whole family of them at one point? Little cubs wrestling on the grass and fighting over the bones. Cute.'

'Did it not seem unnatural to you though?' I was unsure what I was driving at.

'Honestly, mate, I didn't think about it. I was just living my

142

life. When you look back, everything seems like a sign. A clue. But really, were we ever thinking about anything more than how we were going to pay the fucking rent?'

We'd always had this dynamic: speculator and pragmatist. 'After everyone left, their screeching used to drive me mad,' I said. 'Sounds way too human. Eerie.'

'Worse later, when people started trapping them and the trap didn't kill them outright.' I could remember hearing a trapped fox yelping itself hoarse through the night. When I left my flat the next morning I found the trap, with just a leg in its jaws; a trail of blood leading away to the smashed window of an abandoned, half-buried car. The fox inside was already dead. It had gnawed off its own leg trying to escape but had only made it twenty feet. Malik continued: 'Don't have to worry about eating fox meat now, though, do you? With your sugar mummy to look out for you.' I paused, pint halfway to my lips. Malik grimaced. 'Too soon?'

'Why are you so obsessed with her?' I said.

'It's not her. I just don't like who you're pretending to be.'

'What do you mean?'

'All this holier-than-thou bullshit. Like you're suddenly above ...' He paused and gestured, wide, with a flat palm. 'I know who you are, Ellis.' He shrugged. 'What happens when she suddenly decides that the sun doesn't shine out of your arse, after all?'

For all my objections, a couple of pints in, I could feel that it was starting to bother me as well. It was precarious, undoubtedly. My part in our partnership was entirely contingent. Yet it was this precarity that was making me feel so alive, so energised. With you, for the first time since I could remember, I was

143

making something that went beyond myself. I had been living life in a state of paralysed perplexity at its joyless and crushing repetitiveness. Wrapped up in this was my knowledge, bone-deep, that it was the refusal of every drudge watching prestige dramas in their living rooms, every athleisurewear Adonis pointlessly sculpting their body for a physical life that they had been alienated from for centuries, to acknowledge their essential co-dependency, that had led us to this collapse. Working with you felt reparative.

Why, then, did Malik's words so easily shake this joy? Why was I so easily captured by this idea of self-reliance being ultimately interchangeable with self-worth? I needed you; I needed you to need me. Up until this moment, this had felt like an enfolding, mutually affirming. So why now, with the dull thrum of knock-off Guinness rattling my hot veins, had it come to seem a transaction in which I had got the short end of the bargain?

I had always been interested in this idea that our personalities, that series of gestures brought into coherence by the people whom we hold close, are only ever a product of those relationships; droplets pooling, held in place by the surface tension inferred by the air that surrounds them.

Who are we, then, when the tension breaks and the droplets scatter? You and I had spent the last few months regarding each other, beginning to find some way back. For five years I had lived alongside Malik and the whole time we had conspired to look away.

Knowing this didn't seem to help. As our conversation went on and the drinks kept coming, I was strapping myself to the rack of self-doubt and self-loathing and there was a comfort in the familiarity.

The sun was long fled by the time we finally left. I stumbled, heart-heavy, meandering my way back to your place along those familiar streets. I didn't miss the street lights, not any more. I had come to love the moment, turning onto Kingsland Road, emerging out of the darkness of the neighbourhood, when the towers of the city presented themselves. The vertical farms, lit by the solar-powered grow lights. A shining city, jewel in the valley, now haloed by the easy nostalgia of too many drinks. We all need a sky and a direction to turn towards, flowers in the night. As it ever was, when the Romans marched the road from Colchester to their new capital; when farmers drove their sheep and cows from farms in Clapton, Walthamstow and Leyton to Smithfield's market; when the wealth and extracted labour of half the subjugated peoples of the world rushed into pockets tailored on Savile Row until finally, after two thousand years, the polarities – of people, animals, money, energy – suddenly reversed and the city, overextended from a centre that could not hold, became a rotting monument to the adrenalised avarice that had been its attraction. Now, as my feet followed that ancient path, I could feel that something of that awful gravity had returned.

I let myself in quietly, aware of the exaggerated care with which I struggled to unshoulder my jacket, untie my shoes.

'Ellis? Is that you?' You appeared in the hallway – eagerness, on the tips of your toes, in the arch of your eyebrows. You took me in, puzzled amusement, as I crouched over, placing my shoes in the rack, and I could feel something shift in your assessment of me.

So, as I straightened up, I just came out with it: 'When were you going to tell me about Gino?'

Emotions cascaded impressionistically across your face: shock, hurt, anger and finally, most devastating, resignation. You folded your arms and leaned against the wall behind you, staring up at the ceiling. You sought out my gaze and finding it, as I cringed but – caught – was unable to look away, you asked:

'Tell me. How did you survive?'

*

I'll try to describe for you, then, what I already knew. What I wish I'd had the courage to share with you, while I still had the chance.

I knew about the efficiency of Gino's violence; the light touch he applied to maintain control. And the secrecy that under-girded it. How you became slowly compromised, and then all at once.

As I said, it had started small, keeping a few things back. For myself, at first, at his encouragement. But after the day that he leaped to my defence he began to ask more.

I was aware that others were doing things for him, but not who. Until I might be told, one day, that someone was no longer permitted to help with the sorting or distribution, and when I stood, arms folded at the door, someone would appear to stand alongside me.

But I never knew for sure whether it was his influence or the simple power of self-interest. A twisted solidarity. My life became, materially, easier. More to go around. People left me alone.

Months passed and the urge to ask questions diminished. When I say we were looking for leadership, we wanted the one-eyed man. We all wanted to go blind.

I didn't know where he lived. He never spoke of you. There's something there, for us both, I hope. A silence to speak into.

You always wonder: if the worst happened, what would I do? Who would I be?

Whatever I imagined, I fell short. And you've been paying the price, with all this self-loathing dressed up as jealousy. If you were able to be with him, perhaps love him, what did that say about me?

Malik knew, the hypocrite that I was. My anger at him, at you, is just a way of justifying my impotence in the face of my complicity. Malik is a better person – a stronger one – for not pretending.

We run until we cross the river, Sam lagging behind. Following an instinct, I cut right, down towards the Tate.

I think about how much you hated that place, what it had come to represent. I think of the private security firms hired to keep people out, funded by speculators from the continent, anxious to preserve the collection, but only to prop up the value of their own hoarded works, safe still in the bank vaults of Brussels and Geneva.

They won't intervene, but I figure that if we are still being followed the idea of witnesses armed with weapons might give our pursuers pause.

A pale face appears above us for a moment, haloed by a shock of purple hair, before retracting into the gloom. A peal of shrill laughter echoes down to us from somewhere further down the street.

This other side of Southwark, its ancient history was a subject that never came up between us. Everything south of the river and north of Burgess Park has reverted to its long-established function, neglected to some extent in recent years but quickly remembered, of being the place the city poured into to forget itself. The luxury flats there were only ever partially occupied, and always by those with the most means to escape the city, when the snow fell. I came to Borough Market when it became the place to trade misdirected aid goods; instead of luxury cheese and first-press olive oil, it was snowsuits and condensed milk. And the pubs reverted to their old role as coaching houses and saloons, catering to the itinerant with the same licence to licentiousness that it had always entailed. After the Thaw, when the emergent syndicalist spirit – the farms and everything that followed – gutted the market, the underbelly has survived.

Sam stops, panting, doubled over. I pull him into the covered entryway of a modern apartment building, its plate glass boarded or smashed. Without warning he rears up, sending me sprawling, crashing to the floor.

'You.' He gasps. 'They were after *you*.' He laughs and falls back.

'I thought maybe I was imagining . . .' I say. He holds out a hand, still gasping for breath. 'And then I thought maybe we'd lost them. At St Paul's.' I put my head in my hands before I remember the blood, now beginning to thicken as it dries. I rub at my face with my sleeve and stuff my fists in my pockets.

'What just happened?' Sam says. 'Did you know them?'

'No, not really. I mean . . .'

'Well, I'd hate to see what you do to people that have wronged you.'

'Fuck you.'

'Would hate to meet your friends, if that's what you do to people you don't really know. I had no idea that you were going to . . .'

'What? Defend myself, from someone who attacked me?' Through my anger, something about his tone, a look in his eye. 'Why *are* you still following me?' He shakes his head, looking away. 'It can't just be because you're lonely.'

He shrugged his shoulders. 'To be honest, I thought they were following me.'

I am, by now, completely at a loss.

'Do you think,' he says, 'that I don't know who you are? Ellis, I've been here, the whole way through. Just like you.'

'What do you mean?'

'Where do you think I got my food from? How do you think I've survived? Walking around with my eyes closed?'

'That,' I say, pointing back down the deserted street, '*that* is not me.'

'Don't want me to talk about it,' Sam said, holding up his hands. 'Fine.'

'If I'm *such* an awful bastard,' I said. 'Then why follow after me? Why dog me all day with your stupid errands. Why show an interest in me?'

He looks at me with utter incredulity. 'Do I really have to spell it out to you? This morning, I made a calculation. One that we've all made countless times, these past few years. I was more scared of them than I was of you. Why do you think I've been talking a mile a minute all day. I wasn't always like this, either. I wasn't always scared of everything.'

I sit with my back to the wall and look up and down the

street. Derelict luxury apartment buildings all the way along: bleak in the flat, late afternoon light. One building has a single remaining unbroken window, still filmed with the blue plastic the glass had been fitted with.

Fifteen feet away a chain-link fence shifts and a man shimmies out onto the street; shielding his eyes from the glare, he buttons his flies and staggers past us towards the bridge, he begins to raise a hand to us but something he sees – perhaps I didn't clean the blood from my face so well as I had hoped – makes him think again. He bows his head and scuttles away.

Once he is out of sight, Sam takes a deep breath.

'You turned me away, Ellis. From Haggerston station.'

Again, I am forced to confront the fact that willing myself to forget something didn't extend to others.

'I turned you away?'

He sits down next to me. For a second, the only sound is the slowing of our breath. The slowly receding thump of my heartbeat.

'About six months in. Placed your arm across the door. Pushed me back into the snow. You might have forgotten my face, Ellis, but I haven't forgotten yours.'

I can feel the blood draining from my face. My adrenaline is spent. I begin to feel light-headed; my hands are shaking. 'I'm sorry, Sam.'

'Let me ask you something, Ellis,' Sam says, now more gently, as though speaking to a child. 'Have you heard of the hierarchy of needs?'

'Really, I am. I need you to know that I am.' I turn towards him and he flinches.

'A theory to explain human motivation. It was developed during the Second World War, by an American psychologist. A hierarchy of needs that need to be fulfilled in order to reach the ultimate goal of self-actualisation.'

'I don't understand. How you can spend all day with me, not say a thing.'

He waves a hand, impatient. 'At the bottom of the hierarchy are the basic physical needs: food, water, warmth. Above that, safety. As you keep going upwards more complex needs arise. The need for love and friendship. Esteem and respect. And finally, self-actualisation and transcendence.'

'The worst part is, I don't even remember.' I turn to him and look him up and down, attempting to see again as though for the first time. But there is no flicker. No recognition. 'I don't remember ever meeting you.' Such a poor witness, even to my own life. All day I have wondered at his shifty obscurity – never once considering that my company might have been part of the reason behind it.

'What did you do, Ellis, to the man who was following you?'

'It was an accident.' I pause, draw breath. 'I killed his brother.'

He nods very slightly, reaches out, and pats my bloodied hand. 'There's a problem, with the theory. This hierarchy of needs idea. A bias in the methodology. It excluded the sick. He built the theory around his heroes. Einstein. Eleanor Roosevelt. People who had, in his estimation, climbed to the top of the pyramid to look down at the rest of us. Who cares what people like that need?'

'Why did you pull me in, off the street last night?' I ask.

'I'm trying to figure out what it is that you want, Ellis. What you need. This morning, you told me you want to move on. All day you've been chasing around after something, clearly with no regard for your safety.'

'Why do you care?' I can't help myself: 'Does this mean that you're able to forgive me?'

Now he laughs. 'So that's what you're after? The forgiveness of a thief? I don't think it's me you should be asking.'

He's right. The shadows are lengthening up the derelicts on the opposite side of the street. I shiver, a premonition of failure. Every moment apart from you increases the jeopardy of further disaster, further violence, further regression. I need the light certainty I felt in the morning, waking with the notion that I could finally close the gap between us.

Sam stands and offers his hand, pulling me to my feet. 'Look at me. Still breaking into houses, stealing stuff just to keep it away from others. I don't understand myself, any better than you do.'

'The maps?' I say.

'The other one. The one that ran away. They belonged to him. In a manner of speaking. Right at the start, he took over a big house, on a square near the bookshop. I knew it, a famous bookseller lived there. Wrote books too, tried to give you one of them this morning. Part of what gave me the idea to follow along with you, to collect the maps. You might have recognised him. He walked everywhere. Used to wear a cap that said "Ancient Mariner" on it.'

I looked again at Sam's filthy suit, shook my head. How many others were walking around Hackey, harbouring a grudge? Others I had chosen to forget. If I can't even remember all of the people I've wronged, how can I begin to set things right.

'This squatter got in there early. He had no idea what he was sitting on but I'm a cautious man, I left it alone all these years. But, in the end it was too much to resist. I watched the house for a few days and thought he had moved on, but he arrived just as I was leaving. Escaped down the side return and over the back fence but . . .'

'He saw your face?'

'He only knows the thing has value because I stole it. Stupidity, on my part. It was absolute chaos in there. Fine bindings splayed all over the floors. Ephemera cascading down the stairs, as though someone had stood at the top and shaken whole boxes out. A rainbow of recycled paper stocks – a haphazard timeline of the development of photocopier technology. Looked like some kind of installation.'

How many priceless objects had been crushed under my boots, those first few months.

'I must have been in there for hours. An embarrassment of riches. I wasn't sure what to take first until I found them, hidden between a facsimile of an early map of Peru taken from Cornelius Wytfliet's atlas of the New World, and T. E. Lawrence's map of the Middle East. Think about it. If you can trace the water back to its source. Back through all of our burials and diversions. Control the water, control what grows. And where.'

'So, you were going to sell them?'

'No, I was going to burn them. I didn't want anyone to have them, to hold over anyone else. All these years spent hoarding things, I guess I had begun to see that it was hopeless.'

'If you'd just left them there . . .'

'Yes. Well. There are some things about myself I cannot change. Old habits. Sometimes I feel like those habits are *all* that is left of me. Couldn't bring myself to burn them either.'

I scoff. 'Compared to what I've just done, I don't think you need to be giving yourself such a hard time.' I make the sign of the cross. 'I absolve you.'

'By St Paul's, that was an old friend. Colleague, really. Since I was along with you, I thought it was worth trying him. Thought he might look after them for me for a while, until I'd got clear of that bastard who wanted to get his hands on them.' He sighs. 'A kleptomaniac and a murderer, what a pair we make.'

I look down at my bloodied hands, 'I don't understand. Why now? Why, after all these years, would his brother choose to come back now?'

'What made him leave?'

'Gino, he chased him away.'

Sam grimaces slightly at the name. 'Have you forgotten? Have you left any of it behind? The real question is what brought these two people together. One for me, one for you. Perhaps he was following you, already, last night, when I pulled you off the street . . . Seems like no act of kindness goes unpunished.'

'His blood is on my hands, and I don't even know his name.' One thing is clear. 'I have to get to her.'

'Well, I'm not going to let you leave me here.' He looks up and down the street. 'I'll come with you. At this point, whatever this is, I want to see it through.'

You had finally given voice to the question that each of us had been too scared to ask. And instead of answers, that night as I met up with Malik I turned to accusations, weaponising my jealousy to sidestep the opportunity to confront my own complicity.

And after, a sort of truce. We became careful, treating one another with an exaggerated care that was an easy stand-in for the warmth that had faded with this new knowledge of each other; a stand-in to hold our lives in place to see whether it might return.

I knew that it was absurd to be upset that you had been with Gino. Absurd and petty. There was some jealousy of the obvious kind. But really it was what his presence, between us, brought into play between us.

And so, for a couple of weeks we orbited one another, sharing the same space but never really coming together. I developed an obsession with an archive I had discovered: a history podcast, with series titles like *Blueprint for Armageddon* and *Wrath of the Khans* – hours and hours of meandering narration of troop movements and materiel distribution during massive conflicts at the emergence or last gasp of empires, stretching from antiquity to the long twentieth century.

When you asked me what I'd been doing each day and I said I'd been at the farms or some other excuse, really I was listening to these podcasts, walking loops around Victoria Park. The ghostly shapes of the old beds were reasserting themselves, the hardy remnants of old planting beginning to reestablish itself. Snowdrops and daffodils. Young saplings, low enough to the ground to withstand the high winds, were starting to shoot up out of the mulch of their fallen ancestors. The huge lawns that had been decorated with summer picnickers and hoardings for day festivals had now given way to bramble-threaded meadows. The sparrowhawks and buzzards that circled above the blitz rubble scrub of the marshes had multiplied, widening their gyre to hover above these new hunting grounds.

By the Japanese pavilions, the yurt people. Improbably, one of the yurts had been given over to a sauna. I watched as a succession of men and women, naked as the day they were born, exited and dumped buckets of water from the ornamental pond over their heads. After everything that had happened, this was still Hackney.

I would return to the flat to find that new items had miraculously appeared, with no explanation. An anorak left on the hooks by the front door, a plate of strawberries on the kitchen table. It was indicative of how blinded I was by my own self-deception that I didn't know how to read these offerings: needle or olive branch.

One afternoon, coming back from a walk, I shut the front door to find that you had appeared noiselessly in front of me, an apparition in the hallway.

'Hey,' I said, my voice surprising me with its loudness in the small space. You were strangely still. One of your closed fists was held out in front of you – knuckles up – as though you wanted me to bump it. 'You been waiting for me?'

You turned your fist over and uncurled your fingers. In your palm were two pills, bright blue. I peered closer: they were stamped with the leering face of a clown, with a round nose and a crown of frizzy hair. A crude likeness of Ronald McDonald.

'What do you reckon?' you said.

'What is it?'

'2C-B. Ronnies. Combines the body high and euphoria of MDMA with mild visuals you'd get with mushrooms at a medium dose, according to what I could find on the feeds. Thought it might be fun to give them a go?'

I felt excited about the idea but there was also a sense of resistance; I was scared of what allowing things to come unstuck might lead to. 'How can we trust them?'

'Where were these reservations when I was the guinea pig for that stuff Malik made?' you said, closing your fist and popping a hip, an ironic pout crossing your face.

'Very good point.'

'Probably fabricated in another grotty garage or train arch.' You paused. 'I made a playlist.'

'Well,' I said. 'It has been a while . . .' What the hell. 'Perhaps too long.'

You shrieked and threw your hands in the air, running in little circles in the enclosed space. I couldn't help but smile.

'Let's eat first,' I said. 'Once we drop those we'll lose all interest.'

'Not too much,' you said. 'I don't want to feel all heavy.'

'I don't think heaviness is something we're going to have to worry about.'

We made a salad with grapes, pecans and some cheese that Luna had traded for, and had been saving for a few weeks for some suitable occasion. Watching you cutting away the rind and chopping it into squares felt like the beginning of a rapprochement. We ate with our fingers from a shared plate which made the whole thing feel like an act of communion.

You popped a grape between your teeth. 'I went to William Blake's grave today.'

'While I was on my walk?' You nodded. 'Somewhere near Old Street, isn't it?

'Bunhill Fields.'

'Bit fucking edgy there, I've heard.'

'Spooky by the roundabout, yeh.'

'I could have come with you.'

You rolled your eyes. 'I can handle myself, thank you very much.'

'I know, but . . .'

'You're sweet, but don't start with this White Knight nonsense. It's not you.' I pulled my hand away and picked up a piece of cheese, pressing it into a tight little ball between my fingertips before putting it into my mouth. You continued: 'I almost turned back to be honest, but it was all right in the end. I've been looking at some of his paintings – Blake's – on the feed. Trying to figure out if there was any trace of migraine aura in them. Thought we might be able to use them.' You paused. 'Have you seen them? I think you might like them.'

'What was it like there? At the grave.'

'All sorts of offerings, blown all over the shop. Laminated poems, brass rubbings, caught in the branches of the dead trees. I haven't been there in years. Used to eat my lunch there sometimes when I had a Saturday job at an art-supply shop in Farringdon. Buy a falafel or whatever from Whitecross Street Market and go and sit on one of the benches among the graves.'

'All the best green spaces in London were graveyards.'

You laughed. 'Says something. Not sure what, but it sure says something. Have a look at the painting I just sent you. Tell me this guy wasn't a migraineur.'

A naked, muscular old man with a wind-blown white beard squatted inside a sickle-shaped sun, peering into the night below him which was scattered with tiny stars. Radiance speared from the fingers of his outstretched hand and spilled from the bottom of the sun's corona. According to the metadata, the painting was titled *The Ancient of Days*.

'I see it in the shape of the sun. The scooped-out edge, the frilled halo.'

'I tried overlaying my scotoma,' you said, eating the last pecan and patting yourself on the belly. 'Almost exactly the same shape.'

'Have you had a look at his poems?' I could dimly recollect something about a chimney sweep, read at school.

'He had visions, all his life.'

I looked again. 'What's blowing his beard?'

160

'Pressure change, obviously. It's a gale, triggering his migraine.'

'A storm blowing in the cradle of creation. Wonder if it's supposed to be a solar flare.'

'What would he have known about all that?' you said, with impatience. It had been another one of the theories, to explain the headaches. Huge magnetic discharge from solar storms causing magnetic disturbances so disruptive that they interfered with neural pathways.

I was picking holes, buying time, waiting for a bolt of inspiration to strike. But, as I looked with longing out of the window, the storm shutters for the moment thrown open, the sky remained stubbornly clear. I wanted to be back in the park.

You swept crumbs from the countertop with your hand onto the plate and then dumped them in the sink. 'Let's do it.' Went through to the living room and shouted back to me: 'I'm going to put the cushions on the floor. And the lights have to be perfect. I can't have anything that might spin me out.'

My past experience with psychedelics had been less curated. Chomping bags of disgusting dried mushrooms in a tent as a teenager. Marvelling at the sensation of a toothbrush on my skin, or the crystalline clarity of every blade of grass in a festival field.

So far, since the Thaw, I hadn't felt tempted to pry open my subconscious with anything stronger than approximated Guinness. I carried a hollow feeling: anxiety cut with dread. Ripe conditions for the self-fulfilling, circular logic of a bad trip.

I went through to the living room. You were arranging the pillows. 'I'm going to capture it all'.

'A work trip,' I said. 'Maybe I should be writing stuff down.'

You stood and unfurled your fingers once more. Taking one of the pills, you put it between your teeth; hesitated for a moment, frowning, and then bit off half. 'I'll do half first, see how I go.'

'In for a penny, in for a pound,' I said, taking the other pill and swallowing it down. I thought I might be able to banish my anxiety with bravado. It left an astringent, bitter taste on my tongue.

Ambient piano music played and a video of a huge drifting flotilla of bioluminescent jellyfish was projected onto the ceiling. We slumped onto the cushions and watched the ponderous beat of their amorphous bodies.

'You feel anything yet?' you said, with a nervous laugh. 'Just kidding.'

It was all beginning to feel familiar, the sense of watchfulness that came over you – a determination to pinpoint the moment when things changed. 'When you stop worrying about whether you feel any different,' I said, 'that's when you know something is happening.' We lay in silence, Luna fidgeting. 'Why jellyfish?'

'I don't know. There's something peaceful about them. Something comforting. They're so obviously ancient.'

'There's something a little migraine about them. Don't you think? The way they move.'

'Yeh,' you said, taking my hand. 'I suppose there is.'

'I didn't ask you. Have you taken this before?'

'Hmm, not this.'

A spike of that latent dread told me not to pry. 'Me neither.'

'I used to smoke weed with my parents sometimes. They were of the "better at home than out of our sight" school of parenting.' You made a small, feline sound. 'Nice to imagine them somewhere lighting one up now. Dad boring a polite couple with his stories of Hackney in the '80s. I can imagine him, saying to your mum . . .' You deepened your voice, adopted boomer self-assurance: 'Of course, everyone was squatting then, that's just how it was.'

I smiled, thinking of her, was about to wonder out loud whether they would ever have crossed paths, but before I could say anything, you continued: 'To be honest, I stopped speaking to them after I took up with Gino.' You were still. 'He was very controlling.'

That was the opening. Not the only one you had offered, but the most obvious. But I was too cowardly, because even beginning to contemplate the time I spent with him raised the spectre in my imagination of how much worse it must have been for you.

Or maybe not. Maybe he was loving. Perhaps the person I knew was just the part of him hardened to survival. Perhaps he manipulated everyone around him to protect the intimacy that was between you.

I don't know, because I didn't ask. And the moment passed.

The jellyfish video had come to an end; they hung frozen in the void and the projector flickered. You sat up. 'Need to switch the vibe up.' The music changed – jazz, a live album I didn't recognise. But the way the notes seemed to anticipate one another; how this anticipation and its fulfilment flooded my chest with a feeling of serenity that was totally at odds with how I had been feeling moments before, made me realise that the pill was starting to take effect.

'Are you . . .' you said, breaking off into a fit of giggles. 'Are you scatting?'

I felt like I could extend the anticipation, get ahead of the notes with my own. 'I feel good.'

You lay back down. 'I feel good, too.'

'We need to get those jellyfish moving again.'

'We do, we do.' You flicked your fingers and the video looped back to the start. The jellyfish resumed their gentle waft, tendrils now weaving luminescent contrails which hung in their wake. 'You seeing this?'

'Amazing.'

Ease was breaking over me in waves, but I also felt restless.

I sat up, then leaped on you. You wriggled beneath me, laughing, then lurched upwards and sideways, rolling me onto my back. As you straddled me your hair fell over your shoulders and tickled my nose. Your skin shone. The warmth of your breath, the cut grass and jasmine smell of your shampoo were a piece with the lilting turn of the music. You leaned into me and laid your cheek on my chest. I tried to listen to the soft thrum of my body, to the animal tilt of the universe.

You sat up again and peeled off your top. Placed your hot palms on my stomach, your fingertips finding the hollows of my ribs. Your movements seemed impossibly fluid as you undressed me. Your tongue worrying at the wet, knotted problem of my clavicle, knuckles grazing my neck, and I felt light, desperately light, as you moved above me.

Afterwards, we lay curled around one another and stared at the jellyfish, now frozen once more. I tapped my temple, replacing the video with the image of the Blake painting. The corona of the sun throbbed and the cords of white hair that hung from the old man's crown and chin squirmed. As I stared the squirming took on a blueish hue and a muscled aspect: maggoty – blind, hydraulic coiling livid against the pink flush of his skin. I felt a sense of sliding, with horrified fascination, towards darkness. I blinked and shook my head, the movement returned, but not the decay. Back on the safe path.

'You good?' you said.

'Yeh. Nothing will stay still.'

'Nothing ever does.'

'I just remembered. Blake's poems, there was one about London.'

It only took me a moment to find it. I cleared my throat and put on a poet voice, sonorous and sincere. 'In every cry of every Man, in every Infants cry of fear, in every voice: in every ban. The mind-forg'd manacles I hear.'

'Mind-forg'd manacles.' You snorted. 'Sounds familiar.'

You turned your head into the crook of my arm. I wanted to make something, some work that would braid together my gratitude and bewilderment, my fear and hope. The painting, the poem, the jellyfish – no ideas were forthcoming. Nothing could arise out of the connections because I felt the connections between everything, an enveloping warmth that insisted on surrender.

You muttered something. Three words made indistinct by the buzz of your lips against my skin, but still unmistakable.

'What was that?' I said.

You turned your face towards me, your eyes scanning mine. 'I said: I feel good.'

'Oh. Me too.'

It's so obvious now that you were trying to invite me into something, to find an alterity that we could share. It was only ever the olive branch, never the needle.

*

The next morning, on the ceiling above us, you projected a broken tree canopy. Stippled blue sky. A day out in the park. We were in that afterglow of fatigue and disinhibition.

'The problem,' you said, 'once you get down to it, is that you don't really know what you want.'

'Perhaps,' I conceded.

'You've simply no idea.'

'Or is it more that . . .' I had begun to articulate a thought before it was fully formed. Before I had the chance to consider whether I wanted to articulate it at all.

'Is it what?' you said, brushing aside my hesitation. Impatient, as ever, to get to the heart of things. 'What?'

'Perhaps it's more that I thought – more that I had hoped – that you might.'

You were silent and still. What, after all, is there to say to *that*.

'I love you,' I said, miserably, for the first time. 'I know that much.'

'Love.' You turned the word over in your mouth like a plum stone. 'Way you're looking at me. Like you might sooner eat me.'

Stung, I switched gears. 'What's wrong,' I said. 'With a little appetite?'

I rolled over and closed the distance between us.

But after that night together, we weren't ever able to recapture that disinhibition.

Infidelity would have been better, been easier for me to explain to you than my abandonment of what we had begun to cultivate together.

Several nights later, as we were eating dinner, you put down your fork.

'Ellis. Tell me. What is going on. What has changed?'

'Nothing has changed. I don't know. I can't explain.'

You took up your fork and began to push your food around. 'Do we need to talk about it? About him? What do you need to know?'

'It's not . . .' I trailed off. 'I don't need to know about any of that.'

'What then? What has changed?'

'It's not the fact that you were with him, it's . . . I thought I could put everything that happened behind me. Forget it.'

'And now?'

'Now, maybe I – I think that maybe we – can't.'

You sighed. 'You're a coward, Ellis.'

I couldn't explain to you, then. I convinced myself it wasn't a matter of bravery or blame. It was dreamless nights and intrusive thoughts. It was the future that was. I opened my mouth to speak but couldn't find a way to put it into words. Instead I asked: 'What made you come to the church that day, with Malik? Surely you had joined the dots, knew who he was.'

'Of course I knew. I was curious. Curious to see what he had made of himself. Curious, too, to see what would happen if you joined the dots, between me and him. I know you have questions. I don't understand why you can't bring yourself to ask them. I don't know where we go from here, if you don't.' You shook your head. 'What was the point, of surviving all of that, if that's all it ever was? Survival?'

I didn't know what to say, so I didn't say anything

'It's a kind of vanity, I think.' Your voice softer, definitive.

'You think I'm vain?'

'What is it, if not vanity? This *preening* self-consciousness.'

'That's easy for you to say, with your adoring fans.'

'Is that what it is then? Jealousy? Not for Gino, but for . . . what?' You sat back, angry now. 'I'm sorry if you feel that the world doesn't *value* you as it should. That you're not getting your *due*.'

I wasn't ready to hear it. 'You're not listening.'

'*I'm* not listening? You're not listening, Ellis. I want someone who makes my life bigger. After everything we've been through. I can't be the one that always bears you up.'

'I love you, Luna.' The second time I had said it, but again it carried the wrong cadence. More like a defence than a declaration. An end, rather than a beginning.

We staggered on for a few weeks, in an ever-widening orbit. Waiting, I suppose, for the arrival of an opportunity for rapprochement which never arrived. You left me the flat, moved to a well-preserved Georgian mansion in Vauxhall called Brunswick House that had been a bar and restaurant before the Freeze. During the Thaw it had been colonised by a load of migraineurs, living together and featuring in each other's clips – something between an artist colony and a content farm. It made for a good backdrop: a lot had changed, but the fetish for original features persisted.

Once the cupboards were bare, I went back to the farm, where I was welcomed as though I had never left. All part of the new social contract.

It amazes me now that I thought it would be easier to drift apart. The first clip you made after you left was non-narrative: a kind of candid day-in-the-life meet and greet with all the other migraineurs. It had a lightness that what we made together lacked.

About a week after you left, I found a piece of paper on the windowsill of our bedroom, pinned with a mudlarked coin.

It was torn from your notebook. In your hurry you had failed to follow the perforations; it was still a little folded from where it had snagged as it tore. I followed the line of this tear, being with your anger for a few moments, before I had the courage to read what was written in your hurried scrawl.

Ellis is: selfish, foolish, pigheaded, insecure, ultimately doomed to be alone.

Ellis is not: ultimately strong enough.

Sam and I follow Great Suffolk Street south, to a car park where pallets are piled into a haphazard staircase that takes you up onto the railway line. I am done with sightseeing.

We walk westwards in silence, and I anxiously mark the fading of the light by the lengthening shadows thrown by saplings pushing up through the gravel that line the trackway. I resist the urge to check your feed. There is nothing there that can help me now.

I take, from my pocket, the piece of paper that you pinned on the windowsill the day you left. It is coming to pieces now, at the folds, and the paper is shiny with wear. I run a finger over the words. Foolish. Pigheaded. Insecure.

A new mantra. It is time to do away with the old one, time to stop wishing myself into being, instead to come to terms with what I've become. It has taken this sickness, this object lesson in my body's contingency to realise that it is not strength but an access to vulnerability that I had lacked. That I was peevish and brittle in protection of a version of myself that had died the moment the snow began to fall.

'You never did really explain,' Sam finally says, panting slightly with the increased pace. 'What it was that you did to make her leave?'

I considered it. 'It wasn't one thing.'

'Never is.'

'I couldn't find a way back, to the person that I was. I blamed her.'

'Well, there's your first mistake.'

'What do you mean?'

'Nothing lasts. Thank God.' He laughed, then paused, to catch his breath. 'What will you say to her?'

'I'll tell her I'm sorry.'

He nodded. 'Sounds like a good place to start.'

The snow had only just begun to melt when Gino disappeared. Left Haggerston station and never returned.

You remember what it was like. The Freeze in reverse, in every sense. The chaos of all that repressed energy, unstoppered. That night there was a party. Someone made a kind of effigy of him, propped it on a chair at the centre of it, a drink in his hand.

I realise now that I didn't know him at all. I think none of us did; we didn't want to. But as much as our lack of curiosity was a function of our fear of him, it also arose out of a fear of what might happened if he left. It wasn't so much that he told us what to do, but that he offered us permission, to place our needs above others. When the snow melted, someone – a braver person than me – must have seen that we were done with that permissiveness and sought to erase it.

Were you still with him, then? Did you love him? Do you miss him? These were the first thoughts that formed, when Malik told me about you both.

How is it, that we can grow used to these disappearances? Your parents, mine. All of which is to say the two words I should have said from the start. I'm sorry.

Luna, my lacuna, the hole in my heart. Absence made of light. Let's not allow this to be another.

If he can reinvent himself, re-emerge as something new, in service of nothing else than his own supremacy, then why can't we do the same? Not for ourselves, but for each other.

We are arriving at Waterloo, have been arriving for some time. I had forgotten how utterly enormous it is. Moments like this still have the capacity to shock. The last time I was here, the trains were still running. Nothing more terminal than an abandoned terminus. As we drift through the arcade there are still a few ragged, faded adverts: for the opening of the Elizabeth Line; for a musical that must never have opened; for a paperback, a sizzling summer romance. A huge section of the ceiling has fallen in, a tangle of twisted steel completely obscuring the mezzanine where I'd had my first vegan sausage roll. It must have been brought down by the weight of the accumulated snow. You still occasionally encountered this ghost of it, in the shock of the destruction that it has caused. It is these rare moments that put me in mind of the beginning of the Freeze. When time slowed and events accelerated, and we all existed in a state of electrified alertness. It couldn't last.

I stopped paying attention. The glare of the snow was unforgiving.

It was a tiny yellow flower I noticed first. A frilled cup spilling its sunshine out of the tarmac by the railings of Stonebridge Gardens, opposite the Welly, one morning when I was walking back from the distribution centre. I didn't mention it to anyone, as though its presence, and the hope it had seeded, might not survive its acknowledgement. A quick search of the feeds supplied the name: winter aconite. First herald of spring.

A week later came a spray of cow parsley: a sad phalanx of spearheaded leaves, yellow and limp. And then another. A crown of tight, white blooms was beginning to unfurl from the first. I paused at the rails, the peeling black paint sharp under my fingers. Dandelions too, leaves radiating across the trampled earth. As I turned, I caught the eye of a co-conspirator conniving at renewal. I didn't recognise him and instinctively turned to hurry away, but before I did, he smiled.

A month on, the froth had spread: white spumes of wild carrot and hogweed alongside spindles of garlic mustard and tender nettle. And each time I returned to the railings it seemed as though the crowd had thickened: a host of stunned people, turning their faces towards the sun and what it wrought.

These hardy bastards that had escaped the crush of concrete, the lick of poison, the drive for order and control, the great wedge that we had whittled out of the world.

By the time the poppies burst open, and the trumpet blooms of the bindweed had wound their piano-wire tendrils through the verdant wash; by the time the first storms had strobed their way across the grey matter of migraineurs, made matchsticks of the rotting trees lining Kingsland Road; by the time the dormancy had been coaxed from courgettes, tomatoes, lettuce, potatoes in the vertical farms as it had from the wild flowers in the forgotten gardens, parks and alleys; by the time sickness had drawn the solidarity like plasma from trauma-hardened marrow of all of us who had survived; by the time change returned and came to stay, we had begun the work of remembering who we were.

London has always been a city where the winters are to be endured: the season when all the hard edges that we had made were most visible. It felt like it would never end, until spring arrived mythic, whispering greenly out of the ground.

We climb off the tracks at Vauxhall and exit through the station. We follow the bus station to an area of scrub, dominated by three raised billboards. Each had a UNICEF ad, totally obscured by the familiar slogan: SOLIDARITY NOT CHARITY. Brunswick House was opposite, impossibly quaint nestled among the glass and steel.

'Where will you go?' I ask.

He smiled and shrugged. 'I'll go back. Open up the doors, let people in, see what happens. I don't think I'll have any more trouble after what you did to his friend. And I've been hoarding things for far too long, clearly. Staggering on, fearfully. So, it will be a fresh start, of sorts.'

'For both of us, then.'

'For both of us.'

I rub my hands on my thighs. Can you forgive me? For slipping away. For betraying the attempt. I have to hope that you will.

I hold out my arm. We both stop.

'I'll go on from here,' I say, 'if you don't mind.'

'Don't worry, I'll stay out of sight.'

I hesitate, consider one more apology. But Sam is right. I am looking for forgiveness in the wrong place. It has been easier to be open with a person I barely knew than it ever was with you. 'Goodbye, then.'

Sam waves, leaning against the base of the billboards.

Smaller, smaller, smaller. I need to shrink from the account I've made of myself; I need to make of myself a phrase, something pliable that quivers with the present moment. Something unfinished.

When we found each other, I thought I wanted to be held fast to that earlier version of myself that you helped to recall, the version that had a claim to blamelessness.

But I know now, perhaps too late, that when you are in love – real love – you are endlessly unformed, infinitely inchoate. Nothing of story, nothing so heavy as consistency can withstand the relentless heat and light of desire that has reached that stable, self-sustaining pitch of two people who wake up each day to fall towards one another, to burn the pith of themselves to make each other new.

I reach out my hand, and knock.

Acknowledgements

When I started writing *Migraine*, I set out to explore one chronic condition, only to be overtaken by another. So firstly, I'd like to express my enduring gratitude to everyone who has supported me through the abyss of Long COVID: to Antony, Cat, Dan, Emma, Enya, Forest, Jason, Oisín, So and Tash at Burley Fisher and Jake and Will at Peninsula for making it possible for me to write the book, exhausted, under a pile of hats. To K. at City & Hackney COVID Rehabilitation Service, thank you for your encouragement and understanding.

Thank you to my friends and family who read and otherwise helped shape the book: Ned Beauman, Gabriel Bier Gislason, Kit Caless, Jake Franklin, Dan Fuller, Will Harris, Ned Hodge, Antony Hurley, Tony Fisher, Liz Fisher-Frank, Emma Glass, So Mayer, Olivia Sudjic and Will Rees. Thank you to Caius for the clowns (!) and to Antony for the isobars. Thank you to Iain Sinclair for being an inspiration and a good sport.

Thank you to Matthew Turner for helping me take the first baby steps and to James Gurbutt for his patience, crucial structural advice and for saving me from myself! Thank you to David Bamford for the astute copy edits and to Sarah Castleton, Lucy

Martin, Lilly Cox and Alice Watkin at Corsair for bringing the book to life. Thank you to Jonathan Gibbs for the beautiful woodcut that adorns the cover, and which offers some shred of visual coherence to the obscurity of migraine. Thank you to Charlotte Stroomer for transforming the woodcut into a handsome jacket.

Thank you to Hamish for the indiscriminate laughter, and to Ruth and Mary for being the most gracious and entertaining hosts at Hawthornden Writers Retreat. Thank you to Courtney, Jill, Kate and Matthew for an unforgettable month, and for your continued friendship and support.

Thank you to everyone who put me up while I wrote: to Dan and Laurie for a beautiful week in Antrim, spent writing in the lap of Slemish; to Gabriel for giving me a bed in Paris; to my dad and Liz for everything.

And finally thank you to Lucy, for filling my life with light and for giving me Dylan. This book is dedicated to both of you.